RIDE THE
WILD COUNTRY

Center Point
Large Print

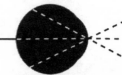

**This Large Print Book carries the
Seal of Approval of N.A.V.H.**

RIDE THE WILD COUNTRY

Cliff Farrell

CENTER POINT LARGE PRINT
THORNDIKE, MAINE

First US edition: Doubleday & Company, Inc. First UK edition: Ward, Lock.

The text of this Large Print edition is unabridged. In other aspects, this book may vary from the original edition. Printed in the United States of America on permanent paper. Set in 16-point Times New Roman type.

ISBN: 978-1-68324-285-7 (hardcover) ISBN: 978-1-68324-289-5 (paperback)

Library of Congress Cataloging-in-Publication Data

Names: Farrell, Cliff, author.
Title: Ride the wild country / Cliff Farrell.
Description: Center Point Large Print edition. | Thorndike, Maine : Center Point Large Print, 2017.
Identifiers: LCCN 2016050629| ISBN 9781683242857
 (hardcover : alk. paper) | ISBN 9781683242895 (pbk. : alk. paper)
Subjects: LCSH: Large type books. | GSAFD: Western stories.
Classification: LCC PS3556.A766 R527 2017 | DDC 813/.54—dc23
LC record available at https://lccn.loc.gov/2016050629

RIDE THE
WILD COUNTRY

Chapter One

Webb Jernegan snugged his worn poncho tighter around his shoulders as he rode with Elias Barnes into a squalid settlement that crouched along the shore of a bay where ships lay at anchor.

They were plainsmen, hollow-eyed and weather-burned after a long, hard journey, and this cold and foggy coast seemed alien and hostile to them.

"First, you fry like a chicken in a skillet," Webb said. "Then you shiver. What kind of a place is this California?"

Elias sighed. "I been wishin' ever since we crossed South Pass that we was back in Santa Fe or Taos, settin' in a cantina with one of them stone mugs of *aguardiente* in my fist, watchin' the gals dance an' click the castanets."

"This is not the time to bring up the better things of life," Webb said.

"I can wish, can't I?"

"And so can I. Keep talking about Taos and I'll wish you farther away than that. Timbuktu, or worse."

"I had no yearnin' for this ride right from the jump," Elias grumbled. "It's a fool's errand. A thousand miles an' half as much more, just because somebody thinks he saw a man alive

7

who's likely dead. I opposed it right from the start. You know I did, Webb Jernegan."

It was Webb's turn to sigh. "You did that. Every step of the way. Every weary step."

"What'll we do, even if we find him?" Elias demanded.

"Take him back with us. I've told you that."

"That," Elias snorted, "will take some doin'. I've told you that, too."

"You've told me," Webb said. "A thousand times."

He eyed the settlement through whose crooked, muddy streets they were riding. The straggling structures were, for the most part, formed of adobe, but there were a few frame houses built in the pretentious, gabled, gingerbread style of eastern states. Others were balconied, with iron-grilled windows in the manner of the deep South. The walls of a mission church stood on a sand hill overlooking the community. Its white stucco needed patching.

The inhabitants also covered a wide range. This was Mexican territory, but there seemed to be few *californios* around. The majority were Americans. These stacked up as a rough, hardy lot. However, some of them were well dressed and evidently prosperous. All—gentleman or ruffian—carried at least one pistol in sight.

"What is it they call this place?" Elias asked.

"The Spanish call it Yerba Buena," Webb said.

"That's the name of these weeds growing on the sand hills around here. They told us at Sutter's Fort that the Americans call it San Francisco after this bay we're looking at, and the mission church."

Elias gazed at smock-clad men in pigtails who shuffled past bearing heavy burdens on their backs. "Look!" he exclaimed. "By glory, they must be Chinee! I never saw a Chinee for real before. An' there's a Chinee gal! Wearin' pants, so help me! A genuine heathen! She ought to be stoned."

"You be the one to cast the first stone," Webb said. But he gazed also. He, too, had never before seen an Oriental.

Leading the Indian pony that carried their meager pack, they rode to the waterfront where plank landings and quays extended into the bay. This was the heart of the settlement. Trading posts and ship chandleries fronted on the *embarcadero*, along with taverns and fandango halls and boarding-houses for sailors.

Webb peered, fascinated, at vessels that lay anchored in the bay. They were gray shapes in the thin fog that drifted on the cold breeze.

Elias was gazing also. "One of 'em's a sloop-o'-war," he said uneasily. "Flyin' the American flag."

"I guess we know what she's doing here," Webb said.

"The most o' the other vessels are whalers," Elias said. "There's three of 'em, layin' off to

9

larboard—that's to the left for landlubbers like you. You'll smell 'em, once we get downwind a bit more. They stink for miles. Bedford men aboard, most likely. Looks like this port's an outfittin' point for whalers. That craft layin' abeam the quay is no whaler, though. A clipper, she is. Baltimore-built, by the way she's raked. That one's a China trader most likely."

Webb stood up in the stirrups. "Clipper," he repeated admiringly. "Now that's a sight. She looks like she's moving."

"She does that," Elias said. His deep voice carried sudden wistful nostalgia. "All clippers look like they're under way, even with their mudhooks down. They're smart ships."

"China trader," Webb murmured. "Now, wouldn't that be something. A man could see what the other side of the world looks like."

"Stick to your mountains and your plains, boy," Elias said, disturbed. "You're not meant for the sea."

"I never saw deep-water ships before," Webb said. "I never smelled salt water until now."

"Twice I sailed as a boy out o' Bedford on whalers for South Atlantic waters," Elias said. "I want no more of it. I've seen the black Africa coast. Set foot on it. Seen jungles an' jungle people. I'll take the plains. The ocean's salt is made up of the tears o' widows, waitin' for men who never came back. The sea's a lonely place."

"Lonelier than the plains?" Webb asked. "Lonelier than a mountain pass with winter coming on? Lonelier than the life we've led these three years? Skulking in Mexican territory; eking out a living. Waiting, scheming for a chance to help my brother and never finding it. Remember the bones we found in that wagon train the Comanches wiped out south of the Arkansas? Men's bones. Women's bones. Could anything be lonelier than that?"

"At least their bones was still on the face of the green earth," Elias said. "But there're no graves in the sea."

Webb looked at an anchored ship that a thinning of the fog made clearer of detail. A lighter lay alongside, from which casks and barrels were being hoisted to the deck in slings. The creaking of blocks and the voices of sailors echoed in the misty afternoon. Twilight was not far away.

"Now there's a sea ghost if I ever seen one," Elias said. "A Yankee-built square-rigger, but with heathen eyes painted on the bow. There's an oriental rake to her spars an' the set of her yards, I tell you now. She's neither fish nor fowl."

"She hasn't seen paint in many a moon and that's for sure," Webb said.

"She's likely held together by the oakum in her seams an' the prayers o' the crew," Elias said. "She's takin' on water an' grub for a long voyage, an' makin' ready to sail right soon by the looks.

Why, she's even had womenfolk on board. That's enough to hoodoo any ship. But the ladies are comin' ashore by the looks."

A small boat was putting out from the side of the ancient tramp vessel and heading for the *embarcadero*. Two seamen manned the sweeps. The craft carried three passengers, two of whom were feminine.

Webb ran a palm over the three-day growth of dark brown beard that stubbled his jaws. His eyes were red-rimmed from sun glare, for they had reached this chill coastal climate only a few hours previously, after days of crossing the valley of the Rio Sacramento, where the first strong heat of summer was setting in.

Beyond the valley were the peaks of the Sierra Nevada where their horses had waded hock-deep in snow, breaking the first trail of spring through a high pass. Beyond the mountains were the many overnight campfires they had built. This was the finish of two months of hard travel.

"First we'll take care of the horses," he said. "Then ourselves."

"I can't say I'd be keen on bumpin' into Sid Raines right at this minute," Elias admitted. "My belly's empty clean down into my boots. I'm sun-blind, travel-sick an' I got saddle burrs." He looked around at the foggy settlement. "Anyway, 'tain't possible he'd come to such a place."

"On the contrary, it's a very likely place for

12

him," Webb said. "We had to hide in Mexican territory, didn't we? So did he. He figured we'd stick around Taos and Santa Fe, for we knew that territory. He was right. He didn't expect that anyone, least of all us, would ever find him way out here."

Elias was unconvinced. "He'd never have come here. We've traveled a fur piece for nothin'."

"You act like you *hope* he won't be here," Webb said.

Elias considered that for a moment. "Maybe so," he said. "For your sake."

"For my sake?"

"I ain't exactly a soft man, Webb," Elias said. "Nor a forgivin' one. The hot blood of vengeance runs in me, too. But you've let it harden you into iron. You've become a man with only one purpose in life, one trail to follow. All you want is to get your hands on Sid Raines."

"If that's my aim in life, I've got good reason," Webb said.

"You aim to make him suffer. You'll try to make him sweat for everything he did."

"Yes," Webb said harshly. "That I will do."

"You'll kill him. It'll stain your soul."

Webb's lips twisted in a bitter smile. "That's the rub. I *can't* kill him. That's the one thing I can't do to him. At least not until I drag him in front of witnesses and let them see what he really is."

Elias said dubiously, "He's a brainy one. An' tough. Likely he's made friends here, if he's here. Might have even become a Mexican citizen. *Americanos* ain't loved none atall hereabouts, what with Cap'n Fremont an' Kit Carson buzzin' around. Maybe we can't afford to kill him, but that don't work both ways. There's nothin' to stop him—"

Webb uttered an exclamation, silencing him. They were riding past one of the trading posts— a sizable establishment. Lamps lighted the interior. They could see two clerks waiting on patrons at counters. The length of the main trading room, cluttered with stock, opened through a wide door at the rear into a big, unlighted shed, which evidently served as a sail loft and chandlery.

To the left of this opening, a corner of the main room had been partitioned off to serve as a book-keeping room and private office. Its door stood open. A business talk evidently had just been concluded, for a portly visitor was shaking hands with someone who had been out of line of their vision on the opposite side of a writing desk. This person had moved into view as he ushered his visitor out of the office. They had a clear look at him.

He was a handsome, erect, flat-shouldered man with a decisive manner. His chestnut hair was thick and roached and well barbered. He wore a waxed mustache, sideburns and a trimmed, pointed beard.

Webb and Elias instinctively yanked their horses to a halt. They stared for an instant. Then Webb kicked his mount into motion and Elias, arousing, followed suit.

Once they were clear of the store's windows, they pulled up again. They looked at each other; they were now breathing hard, a wild elation in their gaunt faces.

"He didn't see us!" Elias said hoarsely. "He didn't look our way."

Webb said, his voice shaking with a rising tumult of emotion, "We've got him! We've got him! He's grown a beard. But that was him."

Elias spoke in that same husky manner. "Three years we've waited. An' many's the long mile we've traveled. Blast his soul!"

Elias leaped from his horse and headed for the sidewalk. But Webb swung down, overtook him and grabbed him, halting him. "Wait! This isn't the time! Don't spoil it now!"

Elias still had the wild glare in his eyes. It took all of Webb's strength to hold him back. "Listen to me!" Webb grunted. "We've got to wait until he's alone! Don't give him a chance to slip through our fingers."

Elias subsided. "I'm all right now," he growled. "I sorta slipped my bowstring, didn't I? A few minutes ago, I was sayin' I feared you'd be the one who'd throttle him if you got your hands on him. But when I saw him standin' there, well dressed, well fed an' overbearin', it all came back. The years o' skulkin'. Of not bein' able to go back with our own kind."

"Are you sure you've got your moccasins back on the ground?"

"I won't kill him," Elias growled. "But there's no pity in me. I thought I had Christian charity in me. To forgive is divine, they say. I reckon I'm only common clay."

Webb peered at a painted sign that hung over the sidewalk above the entrance to the trading post. He read the information aloud: " 'General mercantile and marine supplies. Cash paid for furs, whale oil and livestock. Ship chandlery and commission service.' "

He added dryly, " 'Frank Stevens, proprietor.' "

"Stevens?" Elias snorted. "So that's the name he's usin' now? He's got himself set up quite cozy. A silk shirt an' broadcloth clothes. Clerks to do his work for him. That store looks like the biggest in this cussed place. He's done well in three years."

"He likely bought the place with the money he stole," Webb said. "He's likely made it hum. To give the devil his due, he always had a smart mind for business and he never quits working— for himself."

The portly man left the store and passed them on the sidewalk without a glance.

"Come on," Webb murmured. "We'll pick our own time."

They mounted and rode off the *embarcadero*. Finding a public corral they saw to it that their horses were fed and quartered for the night.

Foggy, premature twilight was at hand when they returned to the waterfront, carrying their saddles and packsacks. They intended to locate an inn named El Posada that the hostler at the livery had recommended.

The small boat they had seen leaving the side of the tramp ship in the bay was just pulling alongside a quay nearby. The two feminine passengers stepped nimbly onto the landing without assistance. Their companion, a big, blocky man, hurried to overtake them as they walked shoreward.

The taller of the two women, who was young and slender, was bundled in a heavy sea jacket and woolen skirts. It was the other feminine arrival that caused Webb and Elias to stare.

"There's another o' them heathen gals from across the sea," Elias muttered. "Look at the way she's dressed. Ain't that a scandal! At least she's wearin' a skirt, if you can call a thing they just wrap around them as such. An' see them slant eyes?"

Webb watched the group approach. "Her eyes are mighty pretty, if you ask me," he said. "And did you ever see such skin? It's golden. Like the sun was shining on it. Why, I'd say she's more Spanish than anything else."

"She's not Chinee," Elias admitted. "She's from one o' them sea islands, most likely. They're the worst kind."

The person Elias was denouncing was no bigger than a puff of smoke and looked about as harmless. She had a heavy cape that flapped in the wind as she vainly tried to control it and wrap it around her. Beneath that, Webb glimpsed a colorful, brocaded jacket and a skirt of an exotic design and pattern.

"Quit turning up your nose," Webb said. "She's dressed decent enough."

"Fine feathers to tempt the devil in a man," Elias snorted. "She's a lot easier to look at than some of these susies I've seen rigged out in whalebone and bustles."

"Dollars to square nails, she's got one o' them crooked foreign daggers hid up her sleeve," Elias predicted darkly. "She'd likely slip a blade between a man's ribs for the price o' a pipe o' opium."

The exotic girl's dark, glossy hair was piled high and held in the Spanish style by a great shell comb that was set with glittering brilliants. Her eyes were excitedly interested as she darted quick, bright glances around.

Webb discovered that the other young woman was gazing at him and Elias, amused by their interest in her companion. This one had good amber-brown eyes that were clear and comprehending. She was attractive of face and figure. Exceedingly so, Webb decided after a second look. Coppery golden hair showed beneath her bonnet. Her features were nicely molded, but with strength.

However Webb had the impression that she had undergone much mental and physical strain recently. He saw some of the same signs of past ordeal in the golden-skinned girl. He judged that they were of about the same age.

Nettled by the amusement of the brown-eyed one, Webb turned his attention away, peering for sign of the inn they were seeking.

The trio picked their way across the wheel-rutted street and reached the wooden sidewalk so close he could hear their conversation.

"I'd prefer to take care of the matter personally, Mr. Strapp," the brown-eyed one was saying to the man. "Meanwhile, you must try to find two or three hands to fill out the crew."

The man was frowning. He wore a salt-faded sea jacket and an officer's cap from whose band the gilt letters of rank had long since been faded by the weather.

Except for Elias, he was about the most powerfully constructed man Webb had ever seen. He was perhaps an inch taller than Elias, but Elias might have been a mite broader of shoulder. Both had arms as hefty as most men's legs. Both had mighty thighs.

Alongside of Elias, Webb, with his lank six feet of height and his one hundred and eighty pounds of sinew, looked puny, as did most men. And so it was alongside this man from the sea.

Where Elias was black-haired, black-browed, black-mustached and piratical of aspect with his bristle of black whiskers, this one had eyes the chilly blue hue of skimmed milk, dry, yellowish hair and a skin that was devoid of life. If he was a man of the sea he might have come from its sunless depths for all the color he carried in his features.

"I need no one to give me orders about my crew, my girl," he said with studied insolence. "You just leave everything to me. You and Miss Martinique run along now, and buy what you'll need for the trip around the Horn. I'll settle up with the trader. You ain't had experience with these sharks on dry land. They'd skin you out of your pretty teeth."

"I'm certain my teeth will be safe enough, thank you, Mr. Strapp," the brown-eyed girl said. "I'll deal with the trader. Meet us here later, please. In an hour."

She took the arm of the golden girl and they walked away, leaving Strapp standing there. He gazed angrily after them, then turned and strode off in the opposite direction.

Webb watched the two young women proceed down the sidewalk. He was particularly taken by the brown-eyed one. He had not witnessed so fine a sight in many a day. There was vigor in her manner. She carried herself with spirit. Like that clipper ship in the bay. She had warm blood singing within her, evidently. But here was a person of no shallow simplicity. She had depths. From the way she had handled Strapp and his impertinence, she apparently had learned to make decisions and stand by them.

"Patchamighty!" Elias growled. "Are you bewitched by the sight of a petticoat?"

"Could be," Webb said. "Haven't seen one so well filled in a weary time."

"I'm a-freezin'," Elias snorted. "There's a tavern ahead where we ought to be able to find somethin' to warm our gullets an' grub to fill the hollow in me."

They started to move away, but were halted by a voice. "Are you two men looking for work?"

It was the brown-eyed one. She had turned back to speak to them. She was very businesslike.

"Work?" Webb echoed, taken by surprise.

"Would you like to go to sea?" she asked.

"To sea?" Elias rumbled. "No, ma'am. No indeed! We're not seamen."

She smiled. "That's plain to be seen. But just *what* are you? Where are you from? A long distance from here, I'd say, by your looks."

Webb answered that before Elias could speak. "Hunters, ma'am. Meat hunters. From the mountains."

She thought that over for a moment. Webb saw that she knew he was evading a straight answer. California, and especially this settlement of Yerba Buena, was a notorious refuge for men wanted in the United States.

"No matter," she said. "I didn't mean to ask awkward questions. I'm owner of that square-rigged ship that lies abeam of the quay. The *Goodhaven*. We need a few hands before the mast."

"Going to sea is about the last thing we have in mind, ma'am," Webb said.

"An' that's for sure," Elias stated.

She smiled at Elias. "I'm sure you'd be well worth your pay," she said. "I'm sorry. If you change your mind, you'll find me aboard in an hour or so. We're sailing on the night tide for the east coast. My name is Madge Peary. The captain's name is Jed Strapp."

She rejoined her companion and walked away. Elias respectfully touched a thumb and forefinger to his weathered hat. Webb cocked a critical eyebrow at him and he scowled sheepishly. "Dang me," he grumbled. "I quit the sea to get shed o' trucklin' to blasted officers, but that gal made me feel that I was bein' piped on deck to bend sail ag'in."

"You were tempted to go to sea again," Webb said. "By a petticoat."

"Not this possum!" Elias exclaimed.

"I wonder why she came back half a block to talk to us?" Webb ruminated. He added speculatively, "She wears no wedding ring. No ring at all. There's no need to call her ma'am."

"Let's move," Elias protested. He began prodding Webb down the street toward the tavern whose lighted windows beckoned. "We better get something sustainin' inside us. Such as a mug o' rum and some solid grub. When this thing starts it might be a long time before we get another chance at a bait o' grub. Something tells me, there'll be rough doin's when we tackle Sid Raines."

Chapter Two

They first located the El Posada and engaged quarters for the night. Their cash resources were only enough to carry them a day or two longer, a situation with which they had grown familiar in these past three years.

The inn was no palace, but there was hot water available for shaving and tubs for baths. Refreshed, rubbing their smooth cheeks, clad in clean clothes, they emerged on the *embarcadero*. Foggy darkness had come. However, Sid Raines's trading post remained lighted. A stroll past its windows assured them that their quarry was still in his inner office. The two clerks were busy with customers.

They entered the tavern, wedging themselves into a bench at a table at the front of the room where a window gave them a partial view of the trading store half a block down the street.

The food and drink were rough in quality, but Elias did justice to both to a point where Webb was forced to hand over additional pesos to satisfy the proprietor.

"I didn't figger on feedin' a squad of men all built into one," the proprietor said, glaring at Elias.

The tavern was crowded. All were Americans, many of whom were noisy and boastful. The atmosphere was alive with a whispering intimation of important secrets being passed about.

But there were really no secrets at all. It was evident what was brewing. The names of John Fremont and Kit Carson were being mentioned frequently. Fremont's name, in particular, brought yells of approval, and the banging of mugs on tables.

"Californy'll be part o' the good old U.S.A. afore another new moon, I'll tell the whole danged world, includin' the British," a drunken man bawled. "An' the *Portsmouth*'s layin' out there in the bay to help us take over."

That brought a howl of agreement. Webb and Elias ate in silence. The *Portsmouth* evidently was the name of the sloop-of-war Elias had pointed out earlier at anchor in the harbor.

Mexico and the United States had been drifting toward war for months. Even before Webb and Elias had left Taos on their fast ride to California, there had been rumors that clashes had already taken place along the Texas border. It had been said that Col. Stephen Kearny had been ordered to assemble a force at Leavenworth to prepare for marching upon Santa Fe.

Webb had served under Kearny in the past. He had also met Fremont and Kit Carson when those two were heading west on one of their earlier overland expeditions.

From the talk around them in the tavern, it appeared that Fremont and Carson had arrived in California again the previous fall with a strong band of tough, armed men. The Mexican government at Monterey had ordered them out of the country. Fremont had moved north only as far as the Oregon line and was now said to be back in the Sacramento Valley, and moving nearer Monterey.

Webb and Elias morosely finished their meal. If California and New Mexico were taken over by the United States their own position would become hazardous, for they both were wanted on death sentences at Fort Leavenworth.

They paid the proprietor and emerged onto the *embarcadero*. The window lights of the establishments along the waterfront fought feebly with the drifting fog. They quickened their pace, fearing their quarry might have left his trading post without being seen by them.

Webb strolled past the place alone and glanced in. Only one clerk was in sight and there were no customers. The clerk was snuffing lamps and pulling dustcloths over displays in preparation for closing for the night.

The door of the small office was still open and Webb saw the shadow of a man at the desk. He was on the point of beckoning to Elias to join him, for this seemed a golden chance, with only the clerk to contend with.

But heels tapped the sidewalk. Madge Peary and the golden girl appeared. They were laden with filled satchels and bundles, evidently having finished their shopping.

Madge Peary recognized him and said, "Hello, there. Have you changed your mind?"

"No," Webb said. "Sorry."

She nodded and walked on past him with her companion. To Webb's dismay they mounted the steps of the trading post and entered. He heard the signal bell tinkle. Then the door closed.

He rejoined Elias. "We'll have to do some more waiting," he said. "The supplies we saw being taken aboard that ship must have been bought from Raines. From what she said to that big man, she's in there now to pay the bill. That shouldn't take too long."

They moved along the sidewalk, leaning against a cold wind. The fog scudded above the buildings. An approaching pedestrian loomed out of the mist. Webb recognized the massive figure of the captain of Madge Peary's ship, Jed Strapp.

Strapp evidently had taken notice of them previously, for he halted when he identified them. "What are you two rascals doin', hangin' around here?" he demanded.

"Mindin' our own affairs, an' lettin' others mind theirs," Elias growled, bristling.

"Waitin' to waylay some poor seaman an' leave him with a cracked skull an' empty pockets, most likely," Strapp said. "Didn't I see you two talkin' to Miss Peary a while back?"

"You could have," Webb said.

"What'd you say to her?"

"She asked if we wanted to ship on your bucket of bilge an' oakum," Elias said. "We allowed that we didn't. We don't cotton to them that stand on the quarterdeck."

Webb shouldered Elias away before the exchange became more heated. Looking back, he saw Strapp approach the door of the trading store as though to enter. The man suddenly changed his mind and went hurrying onward.

Webb guessed that the discovery of Madge Peary's presence in the place had deterred Strapp.

He and Elias stalled for time, strolling the sidewalk, trying to keep watch on the store as they waited for Madge Peary and the golden girl to leave.

Presently the clerk emerged, pulling on a long coat, and went hurrying homeward. Webb found himself quivering inwardly. He had waited three years for this moment, a wait that had seemed so hopeless he felt that he had aged that period a dozen times over. Now, with Raines almost within arm's reach, continued waiting was growing intolerable. Maddening.

Elias suddenly nudged him. Two figures, vague

in the mist, had appeared on the sidewalk in the direction of the store. They went moving away and were swallowed by the darkness and fog.

"That was them," Elias breathed. "The two gals! It must have been them. He's in there alone!"

They moved in long, fierce strides back down the sidewalk to the trading post. Only one hanging lamp burned in the main room, and even its wick had been turned down.

The door to the small office at the rear was closed, but lamplight showed brilliantly against the ceiling above the partitions, along with the moving shadow of a man working at the desk.

Webb mounted the steps to the door. It was unlocked and it opened when he pressed his thumb on the latch. He had forgotten the signal bell, and its tinkle startled him.

A man's voice called impatiently from the office, "We're closed for the night. Come back in the morning."

"All right," Webb replied. He motioned Elias to join him inside, then closed the door and let the second tinkling of the bell sound a false announcement of departure.

They stood motionless for a space. They could hear the approaching hoofs and creaking wheels of a heavily laden freight wagon in the street. They waited for it to come abreast. Webb unfrogged his worn saddle jacket. He was armed with a brace of cap-and-ball pistols in Army holsters. Elias carried a single six-shooter and had a sheathed bowie knife on his belt.

Elias wore a fringed hunting shirt. Both had on buckskin breeches, made at Taos in the Spanish style, with bell bottoms that were slashed halfway to the knee and laced with white thongs.

They did not draw their weapons. They tiptoed down the room, with the noise of the freight wagon covering any sounds they made.

It was not until they were a few paces from the closed door of the office, with the creaking of the freighter receding in the street, that Webb was dismayed to hear a feminine voice beyond the office door.

Madge Peary! She had not left the store after all. The two figures they had seen in the fog must have come from some other door. Their impatience had goaded them into premature action after all.

Madge Peary's voice was muffled, but they could hear the words clearly enough. She was speaking tersely, angrily.

"That stone is worth a thousand dollars, Mr. Stevens. That's far more than what I owe you."

"I'm sorry," a man's voice said. "Pearls aren't worth much in this part of the world. Every whaler and clipper from China waters brings them in by the score, with great ideas of what they're worth. I can get all the pearls of this quality I want for a hundred dollars or less. The fact is, I don't want them even at that price." His voice became conciliatory. "I prefer to deal in cash."

"You know I'm in no position to do that," she said.

"That makes it difficult, my dear. Pearls are a nuisance to a trader like me. I have to send them east or to Europe and place them in the hands of a dealer who charges a stiff fee. It takes months and sometimes years to get my money."

"I'm quite sure you'd still make a nice profit on this stone."

"I must disagree. However, as you say you have no ready cash, I might consider additional stones as payment."

"I'm sure you would. Additional stones indeed! What makes you think I have any?" Webb could hear her toe tapping the floor in vexation.

Elias was plucking at his sleeve, trying to prevail on him to retreat into hiding, but Webb continued to eavesdrop, fascinated by what he was hearing.

"If you'll take my note," Madge Peary was saying, "I'll send you the money, with interest, after we get home to Goodhaven."

The man chuckled. "That's a long voyage. Dangerous. Many people who go around the Horn are never heard of again." He added, "Or should I say heard *from?*"

"You're being insulting!"

"Only practical, my dear. Surely, having sailed with Nathaniel Peary, you can appreciate that. Captain Peary was a China trader. A man has to be very practical, indeed, to be in that business."

"My father never took unfair advantage, if that's what you're trying to insinuate."

The man chuckled again. "I wonder. The Pacific's a big ocean, but news gets around, somehow. Even as far as San Francisco Bay."

"Did you know Nathaniel Peary?"

"I never had the pleasure. But there's talk that a Yankee clipper captain turned pirate in the China Sea."

A new feminine voice spoke. "That is one big lie!" That would be the golden girl speaking. She, also, was in the office.

"On the contrary, I've been told that Captain Peary and his crew descended on a native village in the Malay Straits and set fire to it, looted the place and left many of the inhabitants dead."

Madge Peary's voice had steadied and chilled. "My father never let anyone take advantage of him, if that's what you're driving at. He never turned the other cheek." She added, "Nor do I."

"Apparently he did more than fail to turn the other cheek. He stole a fortune from those people. This was a village of pearl divers that he raided."

"Pearl divers? They were pirates! Malay pirates. Cutthroats."

"At least they had items of value that they don't have now," the man said. "Pearls and other jewels. They were Buddhists who had a temple with some fine items of decoration. Such as diamonds and emeralds and a few rubies, not to mention some pieces of carved jade that would bring quite a price in the right market."

"We were discussing paying for the supplies we bought from you," Madge Peary said icily.

"That we are," the man said.

"You drive hard bargains, Mr. Stevens," she said, abruptly reaching a decision. "You have me trapped. Very well. I'll match that pearl with one like it."

"Excellent!" the man exclaimed heartily. "It's a deal. With that settled, let's forget about business. I'll be honored if you and Miss Martinique will dine with me. I have a comfortable residence a mile out of town. I'll have a carriage brought, and—"

"Thank you, no," Madge Peary said curtly.

"And it is I who say no without the thanks, señor," the golden girl said scornfully. "I do not like you."

"I'll bring the other stone within an hour," Madge Peary said. "I'll bring it here, personally."

The two young women were rising to leave. Webb started to move away, intending to find a hiding place for himself and Elias in the shadowy room.

But a heavy voice spoke behind them. "Stand still, you two. So this is what you rascals were up to. Now—"

Webb whirled. Jed Strapp loomed in the dim light from the night lamp. He must have entered the main room by way of the wide door at the rear from the unlighted sail loft.

Strapp's voice broke off in a grunt of consternation, for Webb had snatched out a pistol as he whirled. Strapp stood shocked and flinching, expecting a bullet.

Webb drove forward, head down and rammed into the man. Strapp, taken by surprise, was carried, despite his bulk, against a post with an impact that drove the breath from him.

Webb swung the barrel of the heavy pistol, laying it across Strapp's Adam's apple, a maneuver he had learned in the Army to silence a foe's attempt at an outcry.

Strapp sagged to the floor, gasping and gurgling in pain, fighting for breath. The sounds they had made brought the pound of feet inside the office. The door was thrown open, letting a flood of lamplight upon Elias, who had not changed position. The owner of the trading post stood there, outlined by the lamplight, a pistol in his hand, ready to shoot.

"Don't do it, mister," Elias said. "You're in a cross fire."

"There are two of us," Webb spoke. "Bend down

and lay that gun on the floor. Then back off, one pace. Back off, I say! On the double!"

The man stood peering, startled. "So you recognize my voice, Sid," Webb said. "That's right. It's me. And now you know, too, that it'd be best to do what we tell you. Put down that gun."

For a long space the handsome, bearded man only stood there, as though debating his chances. Then he slowly placed the pistol on the floor and stepped back.

Elias moved in and picked up the weapon. "You're smart, Cap'n," he said mockingly. "You always was. I'd have liked the chance to have put a slug through you."

Madge Peary and her companion had backed away to the opposite wall of the office, and were staring, wide-eyed. Elias and Webb dragged the gagging Strapp by the heels into the office and Webb kicked the door closed.

He and Elias stood listening, keeping their captives covered. There was no sign of alarm in the street. There had been no passers-by to notice Strapp's downfall.

Webb looked at the bearded man. "It's been quite a spell since we've seen each other, Sid."

He turned to the two young women. "Stay where you are, ladies," he said. "No screaming. Don't be afraid. You won't be harmed."

As a matter of fact they both seemed more startled and curious than afraid.

"Poof!" the golden one said, with a toss of her head. "We are not one little bit afraid."

Madge Peary spoke. "And if we decide to scream, we'll do so. You're the ones who must stand where you are. Don't come toward us. Not one step. Either of you."

She held in her hand a derringer. It was a weapon that fired a vicious .50-caliber ball. This was no lady's handbag gun. It was meant for business, and it could tear a hole in a man at close range.

Elias peered. "Now who'd a-thought she was packin' a sneak gun like that? Ma'am, I picked you as bein' a fine lady."

Webb's attention swung back to the handsome trader. A wildness came in him—the wildness he had promised he would never give in to. He moved across the room, holstering his gun.

"Sid!" he said harshly. "You've got it coming."

His hands locked on the man's throat. And tightened. But Elias moved in. "No, no, boy! You said yourself we couldn't take his scalp. Come to your senses."

Webb's grip slacked away. The wildness faded, but not the bitterness. His quarry straightened, gasping. Webb searched him and found a stiletto in a neck sheath and a short-barreled pocket pistol.

He tossed the weapons beneath a cabinet out of reach, and stepped back.

The man, still breathing huskily, straightened his coat and sleeves. "Who are you?" he demanded. "What do you want?"

Webb smiled grimly. "Are you trying to pretend you don't know me, Sid? Or Elias?"

"I never saw either of you before in my life."

"Don't you wish that was true," Webb said. "A trapper friend of Eli's, who had been to California, happened to mention to us at Taos a couple of months ago that he'd seen a man he said was the living image of Captain Sidney Raines of the United States Dragoons walking a street in a place called Yerba Buena nearly a year ago."

"You must be drunk."

"The trapper's name was Ned Jennings," Webb said. "You knew him well. And so did I. He served as a civilian scout out of Diamond Cantonment when both of us were first on duty there. He left the Army to go on a trapping trip with a company of men before all the things that happened to me took place. He wound up in California. He didn't know you were supposed to be dead, and what he was seeing in Yerba Buena might have been a ghost. He didn't know I had been sentenced to hang for your murder and that Eli here had been charged with desertion and with helping a condemned man escape, both of which are hanging offenses in the Army in time of active service."

"If you're not drunk, you're insane," Raines said. His voice was steady and sure. He was calm. He even seemed tolerant and sympathetic.

Webb sighed. "Sid," he said, "you're wonderful. If I didn't know there was no soul in your body, I'd almost feel that you were right and I was picking on you."

He looked around. A small object lay on the blotter on the desk where Madge Peary had been dickering with Raines.

It was a pearl. Webb knew little about precious stones. The few pearls he had seen had been mounted in jewelry or on necklaces worn by women. Raines, in discussing the pearl with Madge Peary, had deprecated its value.

But this stone was beautiful. Cold, perhaps. Lifeless, as it lay there alone. It needed to be worn by a comely woman. Even so, it held a fascination.

"Stick to your guns," he said to Madge Peary. "It's worth a thousand dollars, if you say so."

She shifted the derringer slightly so that it covered him more determinedly. "Don't touch the pearl," she warned.

"I had no such intention," Webb said.

"Who are you?"

"Webb Jernegan, former lieutenant, United States Dragoons," Webb said. "Daniel Webster Jernegan. My mother was a kissing cousin of Daniel Webster. My friends call me Webb."

He looked at Sidney Raines. "*All* my friends called me that, didn't they Sid? Even you."

He addressed the two young women. "This fellow that you know by the name of Frank Stevens is really Sidney Raines. He was in the Dragoons too. A captain. He was commanding officer at Diamond Cantonment and was acting as chief supply officer for the Department of the West. Since I last saw him, he's grown a little more hair on top and on his face. But, underneath, he's still the same. A rat. A thief! And a murderer!"

"Nonsense!" Raines said impatiently. "My name *is* Stevens. Frank Stevens. I can prove it."

"How?"

"A hundred men in this town will vouch for it."

Webb laughed. "You sound as convincing as ever, Sid. You always had a way of making people believe you were Bible-true."

Raines's manner grew even more tolerant and sympathetic. "I'm sorry for you, whoever you are. Evidently whatever happened to you has affected your mind. However, you broke in here by force. Robbery is a hanging offense in Yerba Buena. There's been too much of it. The committee hanged a man for that crime only a week or so ago."

"Committee?"

"The law-and-order committee. You'll learn what it is unless you leave peacefully."

"Now that'd be something, Sid, being hung by

39

you here in California for robbing you, after I'm supposed to have murdered you back at Diamond Cantonment three years ago."

"I tell you I don't know what you're talking about."

Madge Peary lowered her derringer, but kept it dangling in her hand. "All this is very interesting," she said. "Tell me more about it."

"Sorry," Webb said. "It's a long story, and there's no time."

Jed Strapp had revived. But he remained sitting on the floor, with Elias covering him with a pistol. He seemed to be more interested in listening to the talk than in inviting a bullet by offering resistance. Sardonic amusement showed on his thick lips. He gazed in sly delight at Sidney Raines as though greatly elated by new knowledge.

The doorbell on the trading room door tinkled. Webb heard a heavy footstep enter. "Stevens?" a man's voice called. "Air you still open fer business? I'm pullin' out with a freight string fer Sutter's an' just busted a hame strap on a wheeler. I need—"

Raines lifted his voice. "Thieves!" he shouted. "I'm being held up here in the office! Yell for help! Run into the street and yell!"

Raines had triumphant and malicious laughter in his eyes. He had been hoping for just such a chance. He had known that Webb would not shoot him down to silence him.

The arrival uttered a startled squawk. Webb heard him stampede out of the store into the street. He began shouting, "Holdup! Holdup! Frank Stevens is bein' stuck up. Everybody! Help! Help!"

The strident alarm carried far in the foggy darkness. It brought quick response. Webb heard men pouring from the taverns and gambling houses and shouting questions.

Elias, with a growl of rage, took a stride toward Raines, a fist cocked for a blow.

Webb shouldered him back. "You might break his slippery neck," he said. "We can't afford that, and he knows it. And he knows we can't risk starting a shooting match with women around."

He looked at Raines. "We'll be back, Sid. I'm going to take you back to Diamond Cantonment if I have to drag you every weary mile by your hair. My brother's still in a federal prison, serving a term for what you did. Nearly three years he's been in a cell, waiting for me to get him out. You're the only one who can do that."

"If we're goin' to git, let's git!" Elias exclaimed. "People are headin' this way, from the racket."

"Shoot them!" Raines said harshly to Madge Peary.

Webb and Elias halted in their tracks, looking at her. She studied them for an instant, then shook her head. She opened one of the satchels that lay on her lap and dropped the derringer into it.

"*Gracias*," Webb said, including the golden girl in his thanks.

"*No hay de qué*," she responded. "Don't mention it, señor."

"I hope I haven't made a mistake," Madge Peary said.

Webb and Elias raced into the trading room. Men were shouting in the street. A head appeared cautiously in the door. "Stevens?" the man shouted. "Where are you?"

Sidney Raines shouted, "They're trying to make a run for it. Kill them! They're desperate!"

Chapter Three

The subdued light from the swinging lamp was their biggest danger. Elias seized a crockery bowl from a sales display and hurled it. The light was blotted out as lamp and bowl were shattered.

Webb led the way in a race to the wide door into the dark sail loft. A pistol exploded in the hands of a cautious man who was peeking around the frame of the front door. It was a wild shot that struck the ash box of the sheet-iron stove in the center of the room that was used to heat the place. Fiery sparks sprayed across the floor, for the ashes were still alive.

They ran through the echoing darkness of the loft. It was big and empty and smelled of tar and canvas and oakum. The pale outline of an open door showed at the rear. That evidently had been the way by which Strapp had entered.

They raced toward that door, hearing the yelling and excitement in the trading room as men poured in.

"They're in the loft," Raines shouted. "Go in after them."

A deep, jeering voice rose above the others. "Lead the way, Stevens. It's your party."

The speaker was Jed Strapp. That brought a

momentary silence. Some of the arrivals began hooting and uttering catcalls. "Go ahead, Stevens!" a man bawled.

But none of them wanted to be the first to enter the dark shed at the rear, Sidney Raines least of all.

A red glow suddenly flared in the main room. The sparks from the stove had ignited the pool of oil from the smashed lamp. That brought a new surge of shouting and pounding feet.

Elias and Webb reached the outer door and emerged into the wet, wind-driven fog. They ran almost headlong into the wall of an adjoining building. They veered, slowing to a more cautious pace. Even so, they blundered into other objects, and were tripped by clumps of weeds and discarded rubbish. They found themselves in a lumberyard, and they wandered through a vacant lot where unused freight wagons were stored.

They finally emerged on a lane between houses some distance from the waterfront. There had been sounds of pursuit at first, but it had died away.

A sullen red glow hovered in the fog in the direction of the *embarcadero*. The solid jolt of a muffled concussion hit their eardrums. The red glow expanded suddenly to a yellow balloon. Sidney Raines's trading store was burning. Evidently the fire had touched off a store of gunpowder. Fire bells began to sound. Around them they could hear the inhabitants of the dwellings arousing.

They slowed to a walk, for Yerba Buena had other worries now. The wind that carried the fog along with it would also drive flames through the ramshackle structures of the settlement.

They heard the hooting horns of volunteer fire companies and the clatter of vehicles in the streets. The alarm bells continued to ring. The flames were rising higher.

"You played merry double confusion when you busted that lamp," Webb said.

"I did that," Elias said with great satisfaction. "At any rate, Sid Raines won't be able to wax any fatter on what my old Baptist preacher grandpap used to call the wages of corruption an' chicanery."

They circled through the back streets and made their way to the El Posada. The clerk's cubby was deserted, with all the guests evidently attracted to the scene of the fire. They got to their room unobserved.

The chances were that Raines would be on the lookout for them, so they remained under cover there, leaving the candles unlighted. They kept track of the situation by peering from a window that gave them a view of a portion of the *embarcadero* and the activity.

Raines's place was wrapped in flames. The waterfront boiled with human ants as men concentrated on protecting their property. Water was being doused on structures being scorched by the flames. Storekeepers and tavern owners whose buildings might be involved were frantically trying to salvage belongings by carrying them to the quays and wharfs.

It was a dubious precaution, for thieves were taking advantage of this chance. Shouts and threats and struggles were breaking out, along with occasional pistol shots.

Presently, the first fury of the fire began to fade. The fight to prevent the spread of the flames was succeeding. Only Raines's establishment was lost. The peak of the excitement passed.

Webb and Elias came suddenly to alert attention. Madge Peary and her companion had appeared on the quay where the shore boat from the *Goodhaven* was still moored. It was evident they were waiting to be taken back aboard the vessel, but the two seamen who had manned the boat were absent.

Presently, Jed Strapp and the seamen appeared. Elias grunted and nudged Webb with an elbow.

A fourth man was in the group. Sidney Raines. He carried a satchel whose contents seemed to be of some weight. Strapp had on his shoulder a filled sea bag that evidently contained Raines's wardrobe.

The seamen boarded the boat and unshipped the oars in preparation for casting off. But a discussion had started between Raines and Madge Peary.

Raines's attitude seemed politely mild at first. Then demanding. And, finally, angrily insistent. He gestured toward the fogbound bay. Madge Peary kept determinedly shaking her head in refusal.

She took the arm of the golden girl and attempted to turn away and step into the boat. Raines blocked their path, forcing her to listen to him. She stood straight and unyielding. At last, Raines gave it up and permitted them to enter the boat.

Strapp, who had set the sea bag down on the quay, had taken no part in the discussion. He now prepared to board the boat. He paused long enough to say something in Raines's ear, then boarded the craft. Oars dipped the water and the boat faded off into the fog.

Raines shouldered the bag and picked up the satchel. Webb could see the bulge of a brace of pistols beneath the skirt of his broadcloth coat. If any thieves were watching him with the intention of learning what was in the weighted satchel, they evidently thought better of it. He vanished among the buildings down the sidewalk.

"Looks like he saved something from the fire after all," Elias said sourly. "Must be coin money an' valuables that makes that pouch so heavy."

"I guess we know what all that palaver with the Peary girl was about," Webb said.

Elias nodded. "Raines wanted to haul out o' here on her ship tonight."

"He doesn't aim to lose any time shaking clear of us," Webb commented.

"If I found out you was after me, I'd make fast tracks too," Elias commented. "I thought for a minute he was goin' to force himself aboard that gal's ship, whether or no."

"She turned him down," Webb commented. "She didn't exactly cotton to Mr. Frank Stevens on account of that bargain he drove on the pearls. And what we told her about Sidney Raines didn't improve her opinion of him."

"But there'll be other ships," Elias said gloomily. "On land we'd have a chance. A good chance. If he slips away to sea, we'd likely never find trace o' him again."

He arose. "We've got to find him. He might be leavin' this place by saddleback or in a buggy an' be makin' fast tracks. By mornin' he could be anywheres, with a dozen directions to pick from."

"Keep your hair on," Webb said. "I doubt if he's pulled out—yet. There's one thing to hold him here."

"An' what's that?"

"The other pearl Madge Peary promised to pay him. I know Raines. He'd never pass up a profit. He'll wait for that. He likely has enough pull with the port authorities to see that her ship doesn't sail if he wants it held."

Elias sank back. "What if you're wrong?"

Webb didn't answer that. The same tension was

on him, the same bitter fear that he and Elias had failed after all.

Unable to sit it out any longer, they finally donned their ponchos and left the inn. Raines's building had fallen into a heap of red embers, which were being allowed to burn out. Men continued to work the handles of the two pumping engines that volunteers had dragged to the fire. Water was still being played on scorched, neighboring structures.

They prowled the length of the *embarcadero*. There was no sign of Sidney Raines. Webb found himself fighting the urge to move faster, faster. To start running, start searching somewhere—anywhere.

Then he and Elias halted and went silent. The boat from the *Goodhaven* was returning. Its oars were manned by only one person. Jed Strapp himself.

Strapp moored the craft, leaped on the quay and came hurrying to land. Webb and Elias took cover and peered. But Strapp, to Webb's dismay, vanished between buildings a block away, and when they reached the area they were in doubt as to whether he entered a door or had gone into some side lane.

"He's with Raines," Webb said. "It's my guess he fetched the pearl. The girl was wise enough not to bring it personally."

He added, "All we can do is wait at the rathole."

"I got a hunch that this Jed Strapp an' Sid Raines was better acquainted than the Peary girl figured," Elias said.

Webb nodded. "It looked that way to me, too."

They took to cover again in the recess of a doorway. It was a long wait. The embers of Raines's store were drenched to lifeless rubble. The volunteer firemen finally left, with a flourish of bugles, dragging their equipment.

The *embarcadero* became deserted, given over to the drifting fog. The fog seemed to magnify the tuneless creaking of blocks and gear on ships in the bay, unseen in the mist.

It was Elias who now fumed with impatience and fought the demons of disaster. But Webb had made his gamble and was staying with it. He had calmed. He produced a thin stogie of black tobacco from a case containing four more of its kind that he had acquired at John Sutter's fort on the American River three days earlier. He cut it in equal parts with his knife and gave Elias his share. Webb lighted his stub with a sulphur match from a block he carried. Elias preferred to chew his.

The small boat from the *Goodhaven* still lay at the quay, deserted.

"What do you suppose would bring a person like Madge Peary into trying to match wits with Sid Raines?" Webb finally asked, voicing his thoughts.

Elias shrugged. "The sea casts some queer driftwood together on the beach."

"I could figure her being aboard a Baltimore clipper like the one we saw out there," Webb said. "But she's out of place on that crossbred craft she said she owns. How'd she ever come to hire a man like Strapp as a captain?"

"No tellin'," Elias said. "She's got all the lines of a fair an' honest woman. A decent woman. An' pretty. She's got spunk an' sand. But why is a woman like that usin' pearls for trade?"

"Raines said something about her father being a pirate and stealing a fortune from a village of Malay pearl divers," Webb said.

"I wouldn't know about that, but if there were pirates mixed up in whatever happened, that other gal, the slant-eyed one, would have had a hand in it, mark my word."

"You're bigoted," Webb said.

Elias glared at him. "What does that mean?" he demanded. "You an' your big words."

"It means I'm on the side of the slant-eyed girl whenever you start looking down your big nose at her."

Elias uttered a sniff of disdain. They fell silent. The fog bells clanged, the horns growled hoarsely. The fog was as clammy as hands from the grave.

"She said they'd sail on the tide tonight," Webb said, breaking a long silence.

51

"The tide's near the turn from the looks," Elias said. "If they're sailin', it'll have to be soon. But Strapp's still ashore. They'd not be likely to lift anchor without the captain aboard."

He quit talking. Men had appeared on the *embarcadero*. They crossed the street to the quay and headed for the waiting small boat. One was Jed Strapp. His bulk was unmistakable. He again carried Raines's sea bag on his shoulder. Nor was there any mistaking the tallest of the four figures. Raines. He was carrying his heavy satchel.

The other two appeared to be common seamen. Webb remembered that Madge Peary had instructed Strapp to try to find men to fill out the crew of the *Goodhaven*.

He and Elias left their shelter and moved cautiously nearer the quay. They heard the thump of feet boarding the boat, the rumble of muffled voices and the splash of oars. These receded into the fog. They suddenly raced to the quay. It was deserted.

"Raines has made a deal with Strapp," Webb said. "He's going aboard that ship after all."

He wheeled and went hurrying along the *embarcadero*. Beyond the quays the boat landing faded off into an open rocky beach, which Webb had noticed as they had ridden into the settlement before dark. Fishing boats and small craft lay at anchor off the beach. Dories and skiffs were drawn up on the shore, bedded on wooden rollers.

Webb raced among the beached craft, peering in the darkness at their moorings. All were chained to deadmen set in the sands, or to boulders, and protected by padlocks.

"All right," Webb said, examining a small dory that was poised on rollers. "This chain's rusty and I'll twist a kink in it. Here's your chance to use all that muscle you're packing around."

Elias drew a long, mournful sigh. "An' I already told you the sea's a lonely place an' formed of widow's tears. Once we git into that boat I wouldn't put any money on our chances o' ever seein' them little Spanish señoritas dance the jota ag'in in Taos. I know what you've got in mind."

"Hurry!" Webb exclaimed. "They'll be pulling out. Help me! Heave!"

Elias reluctantly joined him. They rocked the dory out of its inertia, then drove their shoulders against it, sending it toward the nearby water. The rusty chain snapped as Elias added a mighty, final shove. The dory slid into the water and they waded to their knees and pulled themselves aboard.

Oars were lashed beneath the seats. Webb freed them and set them in the tholes.

"What about our hawsses?" Elias groaned.

Webb bent to the oars. "That hostler at the feed yard has gone and got himself three horses free," he said.

Elias was silent for a time. "Them ponies are better off than us," he finally muttered. "They're on solid land."

Webb continued to row. The beach vanished in the darkness and fog. The splash of the oars sounded maliciously loud, no matter how smoothly he attempted to dip them. The clang of fog bells and the blare of horns seemed to come from all directions.

"Blast it!" he panted. "I don't know what direction I'm going!"

He let the dory drift silently. They now could hear the creaking of a ship's gear not far away as it rolled in the slow, smooth swells that worked in the bay. Webb cautiously swung the dory in that direction, groping through the fog.

A big shape suddenly loomed up, towering above them. Riding lights showed faintly.

A voice challenged them. "Avast there! Sheer off! Sheer off, I say, or I'll fire. Stand off to be identified!"

Webb made out the outline of gun ports on the ship's side and the shape of a deck cannon overhead.

"It's that American sloop-o'-war!" Elias gasped.

Webb frantically rowed clear of the sloop, and it faded into the fog. He was growing desperate now, and bending to the oars with straining anxiety. A ship's horn was hooting dismally at intervals nearby, and he headed in that direction, hoping it would be the *Goodhaven.*

But the craft that loomed out of the fog was the handsome Baltimore clipper.

"Cuss it!" Elias said. "You've gone astray again. But leastwise we know where we are. The vessel we want was lyin' no more'n a cable's length off the stern of this one."

Webb kept rowing. After a time Elias spoke. "Hold it, boy."

They listened to voices and the tramp of feet on deck. Jed Strapp's heavy tones sounded, issuing orders. The squeak of a capstan arose, along with the singsong of men chanting a ditty while they performed some task in unison.

"Heavin' anchor!" Elias grunted. "Cuss it, they must be out o' their heads, or in a whale of a hurry to think of sailin' in a fog out o' this bay."

Webb dug the oars deep and Elias added his strength to each thrust. The boat leaped ahead. The ship they pursued seemed to elude them. The chanting continued, as well as the groaning of the capstan.

Suddenly they emerged from the fog as though passing through a wall and found themselves, startlingly, in open water with stars bright overhead and the riding lights of ships reflecting from the water. The bank of fog lay clammily over the water astern.

The *Goodhaven* loomed gigantically ahead. It was drifting down on them, moving with the tide. The muddy, dripping anchor was clear of the water, but the sails had not yet responded to the light breeze that rippled the waters of the bay. Fire baskets were burning, suspended from the spars.

With a final surge they sent the boat alongside and found handholds on the hull. There was no outcry on board. If anyone had been on watch for them he must have given up the vigil as useless, once the vessel began moving.

Men were in the rigging, making sail. They could hear Strapp shouting orders. The craft heeled slightly. Suddenly it came alive. Canvas had caught the light breeze.

They clung to the ship, working the dory to the stern, then abandoned it. Boarding the vessel was no problem, for there was considerable fretwork to offer holds.

Webb peered over the rail. A helmsman was at the wheel nearby. The deck was crowded with cases and casks. These were the supplies he had seen being unloaded from the lighter and which had not yet been stowed below.

He motioned to Elias and they slithered silently over the rail and wormed their way to cover among the supplies. The fog bank still lay abeam, but the ship rode in clear weather. The eastern horizon had taken on a faint luminescence. Daybreak was at hand. That startled Webb. So swiftly had the night passed.

The ship crept ahead, mainly in the grip of the tide, with the sail offering a measure of steerage-way. Strapp strode by, so close Webb could have touched him from the crevice between casks where he crouched.

Elias nudged his arm and whispered. "Hatch open. Let's get off this deck before we're sighted."

They waited to make sure the way was clear, then dashed to the open cargo hatch, swung by the hands and dropped into a dark hold that seemed almost empty.

"This lugger," Elias mumbled, "ain't goin' to be no easy ship. Nothin' but ballast to hold her steady, an' from the looks there's none too much o' that. She'll roll an' jump in rough water 'til your stomach won't know which end is up. Can't figger why a ship would come in from Chiny with nothin' in the hold."

Chapter Four

For the first time, they had a chance to get some breath back in their lungs and to take stock of the situation.

"What next?" Elias demanded.

"How would I know?" Webb said tiredly.

Elias uttered a groan. "If it was anybody but you, boy, I'd be right provoked, I tell you now. Seems to me it's a mighty poor time to be tryin' to figger out what you had in mind when you stampeded into this thing."

"Raines is aboard," Webb said. "That's all that counts."

"What if he ain't?"

Webb felt a deadly chill. "Why say that? We saw—"

"We seen him get in that boat. Maybe they put him ashore somewhere else. Maybe it was a trick. He likely knew you'd be keepin' cases on him. Maybe he's back there in Yerba Buena, laughin' at us."

"We'll soon know. If he isn't aboard, we'll go back there."

"How? Don't you know we're under sail, makin' for the open sea?"

"We're still in the bay. We can swim for it."

Elias uttered another groan. "Waugh! Swim for it, he says. I could manage for a little ways, but I ain't built to be a fish. Swimmin' ain't for me."

Strapp's voice sounded on deck. "Get this cargo stowed! All hands! Shake a leg, you! An' you! Step lively!"

"We've got to find a hole deeper than this," Webb said. "They'll be down here."

A torch basket was already being carried toward the open hatch, to be lowered into the interior to give light.

With only that faint gleam to give light, they retreated down the hold. It was mainly a case of trial and error, of sense of touch, of lost skin on ankles and shins as they felt their way along the ribs of the ship, stumbling over rubble and stepping into bilge water.

Elias was feeling his way along a bulkhead. He uttered a snort of satisfaction and Webb heard rusty hinges creak.

"I figgered so," Elias muttered. "I used to play aboard a ship built like this one when I was a boy back in Bedford. A lumber scow, she was, carryin' milled lumber from Maine."

He was hoisting himself through an opening more than shoulder-high above the ribs on which Webb was braced. He reached down, found Webb's hand and lifted him bodily and with ease up beside him.

"Paint locker," Elias said. " 'Tain't much bigger'n

a squirrel's nest, but it opens on deck as well as into the hold. I got a hunch, from the looks o' this tub, the paint locker ain't used much."

They were in total darkness as Elias closed the trap door. Webb moved carefully, a step at a time, hands extended. He stumbled over a coil of moldy rope and collided with empty paint casks. These were remnants of the past. The place had the musty tang of disuse.

They sat on casks. It was impossible to find a comfortable position, for the cubbyhole was in the eye of the ship where all the angles slanted awkwardly. They had already learned, through rapping their heads against beams, how narrow were the confines of their hiding place.

A transom, stained with salt water, began to let in weak illumination. Daybreak was strengthening. Webb could make out the outline of a small door, little more than a trap door itself, which evidently led out on deck.

The flanks of the ship creaked and groaned around them. When Webb leaned his back against the ship's side he had the queasy sensation of having come in contact with something of the sea that was slimy and alive, for the planks seemed to communicate the slither of the gray, cold bay through which the vessel was moving.

He had the panicky sensation of suffocation, a premonition of being trapped here and drowning. And what if Raines really was not aboard? He began to regret his sudden decision to board the *Goodhaven.*

It seemed to him that it had always been this way with him, and with his brother Terry. Such as the decision that had impelled them as mere teen-agers to abandon a life of drudgery as farm hands in Missouri and become plainsmen and hunters. Then had come service in the Dragoons, and commission as lieutenants for them both.

Decisions such as the one Webb had made the time he and Elias and a detail of six troopers had been pinned down in a buffalo wallow near the Little Arkansas River in the plains country by a big hunting party of Pawnees.

Webb had been a lieutenant of Dragoons in a command stationed at Diamond Cantonment to protect caravans from Indian raids on the trail to Santa Fe. His brother had been an officer there also, but had not been involved in the buffalo wallow fight.

Webb had questioned the order that had sent him and the squad on the detail into buffalo country. The region would be swarming at that season with meat-hunting warriors from half a dozen nations who would be particularly resentful of the appear-ance of American soldiers in the buffalo grounds that they considered exclusively their own domain.

Sidney Raines was the captain in command at Diamond Cantonment. He was the man who had issued the order. He had known it was a mistake almost from the moment he had signed the orders of the day. He had known he was sending eight men on a mission that was not only extremely dangerous, but useless. There had been no need for information in the area he had ordered scouted. All that could come of it would be to antagonize the Indians unnecessarily.

Raines had a reputation as an efficient officer. And also a very ambitious one. He had lifted himself by his bootstraps over the heads of other men. He had originally been a Santa Fe trader and then a sutler for the Army. He had been given a commission and placed in charge of supply and commissary, a position that he filled brilliantly, keeping the chain of Army posts supplied with food, munitions and the best horseflesh to be had in the Missouri and Illinois trading rings.

But his military ability was another matter. He was a vain man and sure of himself. With his genius for impressing others with his personality, he had maneuvered himself into an appointment as field commander at Diamond Cantonment, which was the key post between Mexican territory and the Missouri border.

It happened that two headquarters officers, one of whom was Col. Stephen Watts Kearney, had arrived to inspect the cantonment at the time Webb was detailed to lead the scouting party.

Raines scoffed at Webb's request that if a scout

be made, it should be made either by him alone for the sake of concealment, or in greater strength than the detail he was to lead.

With superior officers present, Raines feared he would lose face if he rescinded an order at the request of a subaltern. He even implied cowardice in Webb for questioning the assignment.

Before Webb and his detail reached the Little Arkansas River they were surrounded by the Pawnees. They forted up in a buffalo wallow while the Pawnees debated the best method of wiping them out with the least loss.

To the embarrassment of the Pawnees, hunting parties of Utes, Kiowa, Southern Cheyenne and even a roving band of Apaches showed up, attracted to the scene by the gunfire. The visitors sat back to watch and criticize the way the Pawnees handled the white soldiers.

Webb and his men knew they were sure to die if the Pawnees made an all-out charge. The Pawnees would pay a price and it was only this cost that caused them to ponder. But, with rival tribes looking on, they could not afford to be daunted by a handful of opponents.

Webb singled out the Pawnee war chief, Brass Kettle, whose shield was fringed with the hair from scalps of men he had slain. He wore a necklace made of the teeth of grizzlies he had conquered.

Webb taunted Brass Kettle and challenged him into settling the matter by personal contact. He called Brass Kettle a coward. He said the scalps on Brass Kettle's shield were the soft locks of women and children that had been stolen from them while they slept. The teeth of the grizzlies were what Brass Kettle had found after the wolves had finished with the carcass of a bear that had died of old age.

Webb had said there was no point in many brave men dying when he and Brass Kettle could settle it between them but he knew, of course, that Brass Kettle would prefer to send his young warriors in ahead of him so that they would stop the bullets and die and he would be safe.

So they had fought the duel. It was agreed that no firearms be used. Webb had been armed with a cavalry saber and a bowie knife. Brass Kettle had a long-handled war hatchet with a steel head and his lance and a scalping knife.

As he sat in the dank cubbyhole in the ship, the desperate stress of that moment came back. Webb lived the fight over again, the sweat clammy on his palms.

Brass Kettle's lance pierced his thigh on the first pass, pinning him to his horse for a moment. His saber missed. The war hatchet grazed his head as he whirled. He could feel his boot filling with blood as they came to handgrips.

They fell from their ponies and fought hand-to-hand in breathless frenzy. Webb could again hear the labored gasping of Brass Kettle's strained lungs, see the wild determination in his dark eyes.

They battled in the crisp, dry buffalo grass with the torrid summer sun of the plains beating down on them. Slowly, Webb gained the upper hand. He discovered that he was the stronger. He managed a hammer lock, and forced Brass Kettle to drop the war ax.

He drove the point of his saber against Brass Kettle's throat and held him pinned down by the blade as he crouched braced on his knees above his opponent. His lungs were on fire and tortured, and there was the acrid taste of his own blood in his throat.

Brass Kettle expected to die, but there was no plea for mercy in him. Webb had gazed around in triumph at the onlookers, at the Utes drawn up in silence on their ponies at a respectful distance, at the Kiowas and the Apaches and the Cheyenne buffalo hunters who sat watching—all avid for the kill.

Even his six troopers. All of them had that same glittering anticipation in their eyes as they waited for him to drive the saber home.

All except Elias. It was Elias who had spoken. "Let him live, Webb. He was brave. Let him live."

That had brought Webb back to sanity. He got to his feet and lowered the saber. "It is not true that Brass Kettle is a coward," he said. "He is a brave warrior. Too brave to die. I would be sad if it were my hand that had killed him."

The Pawnees kept their word that the duel would settle the fate of the trapped soldiers. Webb and his detail were allowed to ride away, unharmed.

What the Pawnees did not know was that Webb carried a wound from Brass Kettle's scalping knife deep in his side and that he had lost a fearful amount of blood from the lance slash in his leg.

He was at death's door by the time the troopers got him back to Diamond Cantonment. An army surgeon saved his life. As a result, he was mentioned in dispatches and recommended for promotion.

Sidney Raines had been the first to congratulate him warmly and praise him publicly. And had never forgiven him. Raines was reprimanded for sending the detail on the scouting assignment, a blot on his record that meant that he would not be likely to advance beyond a captaincy for a long time, if ever.

From that day on, Raines had been Webb's bitter enemy—but never openly. He had waited his chance to discredit Webb—and had found it.

Webb's thoughts snapped back to the present. Elias had uttered a grunt of warning. Someone was fumbling with the latch of the door that led on deck.

They crouched in hiding back of casks before the door opened admitting bleak daylight. Someone squeezed through the small portal and stood in the paint locker.

Webb was astounded to hear the rustle of skirts. He lifted his head and chanced taking a look. The intruder was Madge Peary. Her back was turned to them. She had wedged the door slightly ajar to let in light and apparently was listening for any indication that her presence here was known on deck.

Satisfied that she had not been seen, she gazed around. Webb saw that she was carrying a small, shapeless object in her hand. She moved to the farthest point of the cubbyhole, investigated several crannies and finally found a hiding place. She thrust the object she carried into an opening between the deck and the ship's ribs, which she had to stand on tiptoe to reach.

She again stood listening. Webb felt certain she would discover their presence, but she did not. She decided that the coast was clear and left by the way she had entered. He heard the creak of metal as she dropped a pin in the hasp of the outer lock.

He and Elias did not move until they were sure she was gone. Daylight had strengthened so that the light that filtered through the transom marked out their surroundings.

"Well!" Elias growled impatiently. "I know

you're a-itchin' as much as I am to see what the gal hid away there. I'm goin' to take a look."

He probed in the cranny with a big hand and presently fished out the object. It was a pouch of fine chamois leather, equipped with a drawstring. It was what mountain men would call a poke. But the finish on this pouch was foreign to Webb, and the drawstring was of silk and strengthened by a fine wire core.

Elias felt the bag. "Acts like it was filled with beads," he said slowly. His voice shook a little. For both of them suddenly knew what the poke contained.

Webb took the poke from Elias's hands. They moved nearer the source of light so that they could see more clearly. Webb handed his hat to Elias to hold, then puzzled out the intricate knot in the drawstring.

The pouch was lined with velvet and divided into compartments. He poured the contents slowly into the hat that Elias held.

Neither of them spoke. Cradled in the hat were precious stones. Enough of them so that a man would need both hands to hold them all. The majority were pearls. Two of these were almost the size of marbles.

There were a few other gems. Webb saw the glow of red and green. Rubies and emeralds. And the sparkle of a diamond or two. There were four tiny, carved images that he decided were of jade.

But mainly the pouch had given forth a flood of pearls. He and Elias stared for a long time.

Elias finally spoke in a hoarse whisper. "Put them things back where they came from, boy. There's nothin' but misery an' damnation here. Things like these are from the hand o' the devil himself."

Webb lifted one of the large pearls and held it between his thumb and forefinger. Its touch was that of cool satin. It carried with it the sensation of luxury and opulence.

He placed it gently back among the others.

"No," he said.

"You aim to keep 'em?"

"Could be," Webb said.

"Hold on, boy. Do you mean you figger on stealin' these purty stones from that gal?"

"Not exactly. But, if you're being so confounded righteous, Eli, you're on the wrong track. From what we heard about her father, she didn't come by these things as gifts from heaven."

"Don't talk o' heaven in the presence o' them things. It's blasphemy. The quicker we get rid of 'em, the better, I tell you now. Them red ones come right from the pit, the green ones from the eyes o' fickle women, the pearls from—"

"Bah!" Webb snorted. "They're only pretty pieces of color."

"An' worth a fortune or this old hoss never seen purty stones."

"You're right about only the devil owning things like this," Webb said. "They only belong to the one who can hang onto them. Or steal them."

"I ain't sayin' you're wrong. I ain't sayin' she didn't come into them except through violence. The temptation's on us now. The devil's got his hands on our shoulders."

Webb poured the gems back into the pouch and knotted the drawstring. "You and your preaching," he said.

"You mean you're goin' to put 'em back where we found 'em?" There was a squeak of panic in Elias's voice.

Webb glared at him. "You two-tongued fraud! All this mealymouthed talk about temptation and the devil, when every minute of the time you were the one who wanted to keep these pretty things."

"Satan's got me in his claws," Elias sighed. "I'm weak o' will, an' beset by greed."

They went silent, listening to voices on deck. Jed Strapp was speaking. "You ain't givin' no more orders on this ship, my fine lady. I'm the captain, an' it's time you learned that. If anybody's set ashore it might be you. We ain't makin' port short o' Panama, or maybe Valparaiso, an' that's that."

Another voice spoke. It was that of Sidney Raines. "Now, now, Miss Peary! There's no cause

70

for being upset. I'm aboard, and there's nothing that can be done about it now. There's no harm done. Don't blame Captain Strapp."

Webb and Elias were gazing at each other triumphantly. "You won't have to swim for it, Eli," Webb breathed, elated. "He's aboard! We didn't lose him after all!"

Raines was speaking again. "My real reason for coming aboard was to collect payment on what you owe me. You had paid only half what was due, Miss Madge. Or had you forgotten?"

"I sent the other half ashore with Captain Strapp last night with orders for him to give it to you," Madge Peary said coldly.

"Now, danged if it didn't slip my mind," Strapp said blandly. "I must still have it in my other coat."

"I'm sure you have," Raines said ironically. "I owe you an apology, Miss Madge."

"You owe me more than that," she said. "You already had been paid more than the price of the supplies. But now that Mr. Strapp can give you what I promised, there's still time to put you ashore."

"That won't be necessary," Raines said.

"On the contrary, I believe it will," she said. "We'll be on the outgoing tide through the strait into the open sea, but we can lay to long enough to put you ashore in the small boat. Please do so, Mr. Strapp."

"I've already paid Captain Strapp my passage money," Raines said. "To the east coast."

"But—"

"It's all settled," Strapp snapped curtly. "There ain't any sense in passin' up a chance to make a little passenger money. An' I ain't layin' this ship to, or puttin' anybody ashore right now."

Strapp's heavy step moved away.

"Now, Miss Madge," Raines said, and apparently he was following her down the deck, seeking to mollify her. "You're lookin' at this thing the wrong way."

A cabin door slammed. Raines quit talking.

Webb looked at the pouch in his hand. "Maybe now we *sabe* why she hid this," he said.

"The devil's havin' his fun on this ship," Elias said. "That gal made a sorry mistake when she promised to come up with another pearl to pay Raines. Even an idjit would begin to figure that there likely was more where them two come from."

"Especially when Raines had heard about her father's raid on that place down in the sea islands," Webb said ironically.

"On top o' that, you show up," Elias said. "Raines knows he has to light a shuck mighty fast. His store burns down, so he's got nothin' to hold him in the way of belongings except what he saved in that satchel. Anyway he'd already got wind of somethin' worth a lot more'n what the store was worth."

"And a lot more than he stole from the Army," Webb said. "He's out to get these pretty stones." He added, "And I'm more sure than before that Strapp is in on it with him. They got their heads together last night before Strapp let him come aboard this ship. That's my guess."

He moved around the cubbyhole until he found a new hiding place for the pouch. The cranny he chose was at foot level, a crevice between the decking and a bulwark.

"That thing's worth enough to buy this ship and half a dozen like it," Elias muttered. "Or any man."

"Or any woman?" Webb said.

"She *could* have come by 'em honest," Elias argued.

"That's right," Webb agreed. "She could have. She might have gathered them up on some beach somewhere."

"There're other ways. Honest ways."

"Name a few," Webb said. "I'm listening."

Elias opened his mouth to speak, but couldn't think of anything to say.

"Such as her father turning pirate and taking them from natives?" Webb prompted him.

"I don't feel right about us takin' 'em from her," Elias exploded. "I sorta cotton to her."

"*Taking* them?" Webb exclaimed. "Good Lord, Eli! Do you entertain any fool notion that we'll be allowed to walk off this ship alive with those things in our hands?"

73

"I reckon there'd be opposition," Elias admitted.

"That's putting it mildly. These pretty stones are our ace in the hole, our big medicine. Once they find out that we're the only ones who know where they are, our chances of staying alive will be considerably better."

Elias thought that over and found reason to be lighter of spirit. "O' course!" he rumbled. "O' course!"

The deckload of cargo was still being stowed below, creating considerable thumping and banging and shouting in the adjoining hold. In spite of the uproar Elias, wrapped in the poncho, fell asleep. But Webb, though he was bone weary, could not drop off. He huddled in the chilly gloom, trying to keep warm, trying not to think, trying not to look back.

For looking back was dreary, bitter punishment. He remembered the day he had been court-martialed. That had taken place at Fort Leavenworth with pomp and the glitter and clank of the swords officers of the court had worn.

Some of those officers had been comrades in arms in the past. But when it was over he had not been given even the doubtful privilege of facing a firing squad. The verdict was death by hanging.

There had been a girl. She was the daughter of an Army colonel and he had believed he was desperately in love with her. She had never come to see him while he awaited trial. She had never sent word. He had never seen her again. He had since heard that she was married.

After all, there had been no promises, nothing but close friendship. But he had expected that she would believe in him. She had only believed, like so many others, that he was guilty.

It suddenly occurred to him that he could no longer recall exactly how she looked, or the timbre of her voice. She had faded into memory. That shocked him. He realized that he had not thought of her at all in many months. So little had they really meant to each other. His desperate love had been only the infatuation of a soldier in need of the promise of escape from loneliness and hardship. And where was the bitterness? That was forgotten too.

Only Elias and his brother had believed in him. Elias would have been killed and scalped by the Pawnees that day at the buffalo wallow, except for the duel Webb had fought with Brass Kettle. The big man had never forgotten. But their loyalty to each other went beyond that. They were friends. It was a bond nothing could break.

As for his brother, who was serving twenty years in prison as an accomplice in the crime for which Webb had been convicted, the tie was equally close. Terence Jernegan, who was a year younger than Webb, was in prison only because of his blood relationship with Webb. Sidney Raines had seen to that also.

Stowing of the cargo was finished. Webb heard the hatch being battened. The movement of the ship roughened. The *Goodhaven* seemed to be caught in powerful cross tides. He felt the ship lift and her bow began to plunge.

Strapp and another ship's officer were droning orders. More canvas evidently was being unfurled. The rigging buzzed with activity. The ship heeled sharply, then steadied. Her manner changed. She seemed to be swinging in a mighty cradle whose motion was directed by a giant hand.

Webb could hear the musical sound of blocks and tackle creaking and straining in unison, of the wind humming against taut sails and the thud of waves against the bow. Somewhere a sailor was singing in a foreign tongue.

"We're at sea," said Elias.

Chapter Five

Webb listened to these sounds of the sea for a time. He arose at last, stretched and pulled in his belt a notch. "I'm hungry," he said. "Let's get out of this hole."

"What? You mean to show ourselves?"

"What else? We can't stay here and starve."

"But—" Elias glanced toward the hiding place of the jewels.

"We'll go out by the way we came in," Webb said. "Through the hold. They'll never know we were in this place."

"The gal will likely figure it out when she finds the cussed things are gone from where she left 'em," Elias said. "Then what?"

"I doubt if she'd mention it in public," Webb said. "There are too many wolves around and after the same bait."

They opened the trap door into the hold. The stores that had been taken aboard occupied only a small part of the echoing interior of the ship and had been lashed below the main hatch where they could be reached with a minimum of effort.

"This ship is running mighty light, like you said," Webb commented as they lowered themselves into the hold. "It seems like a waste to make a long trip with an empty hold."

"If you ask me, this old windjammer's bound for home with the richest cargo she ever carried an' the biggest profit," Elias said. "The kind o' cargo she has aboard don't have to be big to put the owner on easy street."

They located a ladder that led to a companionway to the deck. They inspected their pistols as best they could in the gloom.

"All right," Webb said. He mounted the steps and tested the hatch. It was hinged and unbarred. He swung it open and climbed into the companionway. Elias came up the ladder, squeezed his shoulders through the hatch and joined him.

Webb led the way out on deck. He could only stand for seconds and gaze.

Around them was the sea. A green sea, laced with white-fringed waves, their crests torn to spray by the wind. This sea was alive! And the wind was something. It was impersonal and Webb had the impression that it was eternal, ceaseless.

He had seen times on the plains when the sky had turned bleak and remote and the wind had blown for days on end. But, on the plains, he had never known this sense of inadequacy, this inner, aching knowledge of desolation. He knew now what Elias had meant when he talked of the loneliness of the sea.

He looked at Elias and saw in him something of this same forlorn awe.

He gazed up. The sails, weathered and patched

and stained, were taut-stretched to embrace the wind.

Jed Strapp's outraged voice blared behind them, "Well would you look at what crawled out of the bilge!"

Strapp stood, mighty legs spread, swelling with outraged fury. "So it's you two again!" he said thickly.

His hand instinctively touched his throat where Webb had struck him with the barrel of the six-shooter. His voice was still hoarse from the effects of that blow.

"Dirty stowaways!" he said. "You're the ones that tried to rob Stevens and set fire to his place. And you, there, are the one that slugged me. That was the worst mistake you'll ever make."

He came striding toward them, his fists knotted. He halted suddenly, looking at the holstered pistols they had strapped outside their ponchos. He sized them up more carefully.

"I figgered last night you was Injuns or Mexicans," he said. "But it looks like you ain't. What are you? Breeds?"

"Could be," Webb said. "My great-grandfather was supposed to have had a Delaware woman as one of his wives way back—"

"I ain't interested in your great-grandfather!" Strapp yelled. "What are you up to, tryin' to stow away on my ship?"

"We came aboard just as the anchor was being

pulled," Webb said. "We saw that you were busy, so we decided it'd be better to wait until we all had time to talk it over."

"Talk is it? Why you—"

"We'll pay for our passage, of course," Webb said.

"Pay? With what?"

"We have some money. A little."

"A little ain't enough. This ship's bound for the east coast by way of Cape Stiff."

"We'll not be with you that far," Webb said. "And we'll work out the rest of the fare, if need be."

"Oh, so you're tellin' me what you want, and where an' when you'd like to be landed. An' you're willin' to work your way. You'll work, whether you're willin' or not, you can bank on that. But first, I'm goin' to have you keelhauled. That'll take some of the sass out of you."

Strapp raised his voice to a bellow. "Biggle! Biggle! Where'n blazes are you? Step lively, man. Turn out the crew. We've got stowaways aboard. One of 'em slugged me last night an' robbed a storekeeper in Yerba Buena."

A gangling, sallow-cheeked man wearing a cap that evidently was that of a second officer appeared and bawled commands. Seamen came hurrying on deck.

"Break out a line for keelhaulin'," Strapp ordered. "We'll give this one a taste o' barnacles.

Maybe that'll teach him not to try to give orders aboard ship."

Webb spoke conversationally. "You don't want to get a bullet in your belly, now do you, Strapp?"

He and Elias backed against the deckhouse. Neither had made any move toward their pistols. But Strapp, about to voice another order, broke it off. He appraised them carefully.

"Biggle!" Strapp said. "Better arm yourself. These two aim to resist. That's mutiny."

"We'll resist," Webb said. "Unless you quit this talk about keelhauling. I've heard of such things at sea. I don't care to learn the details." He looked at Biggle and added, "Everybody will be better off, including you, if we settle this by paying what we can on our passage and working out the rest. Better—and healthier."

Strapp only stood glaring at them. He was determined to pay off Webb for the punishment he had taken in Raines's store.

Biggle took this as an order to go ahead, which it was. He ducked out of sight. Webb could hear him running along the opposite deck, evidently heading somewhere to find weapons.

Webb drew his pistol. "Come here, Strapp!" he said.

When Strapp did not move, he cocked the hammer and fired. The bullet struck the planking between Strapp's feet and glanced in screeching flight over the waves.

Strapp was a tough, nerve-hardened man. He blinked, his broad lips twitching a little, but he stood his ground. Webb walked to him, jammed the muzzle against his stomach.

"Tell your mate to keep his hands off guns," he said.

"Tell him yourself," Strapp said.

Madge Peary came hurrying on deck. "Stop this!" she cried. "There's no need for shooting." Back of her Webb saw the frightened face of the golden girl.

"There's no need for keelhauling, either," Webb said.

He looked past the two girls at a new arrival who had appeared from a cabin. "Or maybe you don't agree, Sid," he added.

Sidney Raines stared unbelievingly at Webb and Elias. Then he accepted the situation and shrugged.

"I don't know who you are, or what you've got in mind, fellow," he said. "But I must say you're persistent. You're the ruffians who tried to rob me and burned down my store."

Biggle cautiously poked his head in view from the shelter of a deckhouse. He had a shotgun in his hands. He started to bring the gun to bear on Webb.

Webb fired a second shot. The slug ripped a

gouge in the cabin wall just above Biggle's head, showering him with splinters. He ducked back without firing his weapon.

"Stop it!" Madge Peary implored. "Stop it!"

Webb walked down the deck and found Biggle crouching down, digging at his eyes, still blinded by the splinters. The shotgun lay on the deck. Webb kicked the weapon into the sea through the scuppers. Biggle scuttled out of sight down the opposite deck.

"Nobody's hurt yet," Webb said.

"There will be," Strapp said. "The two of you'll wisht you'd never been born. Do you know who I am?"

"From what I've heard, your name is Strapp," Webb said. "You're supposed to be captain of this ship. I'd estimate that you weigh half as much as a mule, but it's mainly blubber and bluster."

"I'm *Jed* Strapp!" Strapp snarled.

Webb eyed him. "I take it that's supposed to put the fear of the Almighty in me," he said musingly. "Am I supposed to have heard of you?"

Sidney Raines laughed. "Strapp," he said jeeringly. "Your reputation as a bucko captain doesn't seem to be as widespread as you think."

Raines addressed Webb. "Captain Strapp is rather touchy about his rep. He's pretty well known in some places. Such as the Sundra Straits, or Borneo. You've dealt a blow to his pride, I'm afraid."

Webb looked at Madge Peary. "We came aboard without permission, but we're willing to pay passage to the first port where you can put us ashore." He paused and pointed his gun at Raines. "He's going with us when we leave this ship."

She eyed him. "You and Mr. Stevens have some sort of a grudge against each other," she said. "I—"

"Raines," Webb corrected her. "His name is Raines."

"So it's Raines," she said. "Even if we put you ashore, I doubt if he would—"

"There's nobody goin' to be set ashore until I say so," Strapp exploded. "An' that might be a long ways from here. You've got nothin' to say about this, my lady. How many times do I have to tell you to keep out of the captain's affairs? It's me that'll decide how to handle stowaways."

"By keelhauling?" she demanded.

"That's right. By keelhauling this sea lawyer here."

"You can't mean that. Keelhauling is the worst kind of brutality. It might be murder. I've heard that many men drown when—"

"That's his worry," Strapp said.

"And how about Mr. Stevens, or Raines or whatever name he goes by?" she demanded. "Do you intend to keelhaul him too?"

"Now why would I be doin' that?"

"He's a stowaway too, isn't he? He came

aboard after I had refused permission to him."

"That's another thing that's none of your affair. He's payin' his way, an' payin' well."

"With what?"

Strapp ignored that. "His fare will help meet expenses an' the Lord knows we're short of cash."

She was angry, but also inwardly appalled and frightened by her helplessness. But she was trying desperately to keep up a brave front.

"Thanks for trying to help," Webb said to her. "It seems there's at least one decent person aboard this scow. But this is a personal matter now between Strapp and myself. He isn't worried particularly about us being stowaways. He wants to pay me off for roughing him up last night. He's that kind. No sand. Not guts enough to try to square it personally."

Strapp looked Webb over scornfully. "Why, I'd bust you in two like I would a pipestem," he said.

"How'd you like to try to break the likes of this pipestem?" Elias broke in.

"This is my quarrel, Eli," Webb said. "Stay out of it. Strapp, I'm willing to try it your way, first. Then, to even things up, we'll fight again. My way."

"Your way?"

Webb motioned with his pistol. "My way. These things make every man equal."

Strapp blinked again, his mouth grimacing with distaste. Elias laughed tauntingly. "That don't grain well with him. He don't like an even fight."

"We'll see how proud he talks after he gets a taste of the sharp edge of barnacles," Strapp snapped.

"I tell you there'll be no keelhauling," Madge Peary said sharply. "I forbid—" She broke off, then screamed, "Look out!"

It was a warning to Webb and Elias. But too late. Webb whirled, realizing that men were leaping from above. One was the sallow-faced Biggle. He and other seamen had mounted into the rigging and had worked their way unseen along the boom of a sail, hidden by the bellied canvas, until they were in a position to attack.

All were armed with what looked like short, rounded clubs. This was Webb's first experience with belaying pins. He tried to fend them off, but he had no time to balance himself. He parried a blow that was aimed at his head. The belaying pin numbed his arm, and his pistol dropped to the deck.

They were all around him, slugging at him. Sidney Raines charged in and leaped on his back, pinning his arms to his sides.

Half a dozen men seemed to be battling Elias— and losing the fight. Webb caught a glimpse of one sailor hurtling back, a sick and broken look in his face, clutching at his middle where Elias had landed a foot or a fist.

Then Strapp moved in swinging a club and brought it down on Elias's head.

A moment later the scene faded for Webb as a belaying pin caught him above the ear. He tried to stay on his feet, but numbness struck all through him.

He felt fists and kicking as he went down. He heard Madge Peary and the golden girl screaming wildly. "You'll kill him. You'll kill him. Stop it! Stop it!"

That faded off too. Presently, dreamily, he could hear Strapp's voice, as from far away. "All right, boys. He's comin' around. Douse him with some more water. Rig a line. You there at the wheel. Bring her into the wind. We'll lay to while we keelhaul a man."

Chapter Six

Cold sea water drenched Webb. It drove icy chill through him, but his head cleared.

He was lifted roughly to his feet. He had been disarmed and stripped to the waist. His boots had been removed. His wrists were lashed together at the front.

Biggle, snickering and giggling, was busy looping the end of a long length of line around his ankles. Strapp was directing the operation.

Elias lay on the deck nearby. His arms were lashed to his sides, iron shackles had been clamped on his ankles fitted with a chain that was pad-locked around a mast. This seemed unnecessary, for he lay inert, his face gray beneath the black whiskers that masked his jaws.

He seemed to be dead!

Sidney Raines stood apart, no particular expression on his handsome, bearded face. He had a hand on Madge Peary's arm and evidently was urging her to go to her cabin.

She forcibly pulled away from him and joined the golden girl. She was ashen, almost as colorless as the still face of Elias.

"Get them females off the deck!" Strapp commanded. "This is no place for them."

"You don't want us to be witnesses," Madge Peary said. "You know I'll have you before a court for this, don't you?"

Raines moved, intending to pick her up bodily and carry her below. He paused. She had her derringer in her hand. And it was cocked.

"I'm staying," she said. "And so is Loa."

"Stay an' be damned!" Strapp raged.

He glared at the crew. "All right. Lively now. Bend that line overboard. Work it under the hull to midships. Move, I tell you! You there, and you! And you! The rest of you stand by the line to play this fish. Stand by, I tell you!"

Some of the seamen were only shuffling their feet nervously, sickly expressions on their faces. Suddenly, they wanted no further part in this. Strapp moved among them like an angry bear. "Jump when I give an order!" he snapped.

He swung a fist, knocking a man down, and drove a boot into the body of another, sending him spinning and doubled in agony. He turned on the others. Cowed, they hastily moved to obey.

The line was rigged to a block on the arm of a spar and passed over the prow and worked beneath the hull until it ringed the ship at its waist.

Strapp made sure the line was made fast to Webb's ankles. Then he picked Webb up bodily, walked across the deck, lifted him high above his head in a display of enormous strength and hurled him over the rail into the sea.

Webb plunged beneath the surface. After a moment he was jerked violently downward as the line tightened on his ankles.

The ship was still moving slowly, and this helped rake his body along the barnacled hull. He let himself go limp, trying to conserve strength and oxygen.

He was drawn deeper. The crew on the deck opposite the one from which Strapp had tossed him were hauling on the line, dragging him bodily beneath the keel. This, along with the motion of the ship, and the depth to which he was yanked, created torturing pressure.

He needed air. His temples began to throb. He was taking punishment against the barnacles, but that was minor compared to the agony in his lungs. He vaguely realized that he was rising. He had been drawn entirely beneath the keel and was now being pulled feet first toward the surface. That gave him the last spark of strength to hang on. He knew that if he swallowed water now he would die. So he held out.

Dull lights of sickly colors were bursting in his head. Then he realized that he had emerged feet first above the surface. He began gasping for air—and found it. He half-strangled as water dripped into his mouth and nostrils.

He was suspended head down alongside the

ship. His body thudded against the vessel's side as it rolled in the swells. He choked and strangled, but he was breathing.

He was alive! Agony still knifed at his lungs. The blood, blending with the sea water that drained from his clothes, was the price the barnacles had taken.

He was swung higher and came level with Strapp's grinning face at the rail. Raines was there also. Raines was frowning a little with distaste as though he regretted this sort of violence.

Using a boat hook, Strapp swung Webb inboard. He was lowered onto the deck and sprawled there, gagging, his lungs laboring.

Finally, that eased. At last he was able to roll over and try to sit up. The lashings had been cut from his wrists and ankles.

His heart lifted. He saw Elias. The big man was alive! He was on his feet. He, too, had been freed. The chain and shackles had been removed.

That did more than anything else to revive Webb. He found that a blanket had been placed over him. He realized he was trembling uncontrollably, chilled to the marrow.

Madge Peary and the golden girl were looking down at him. Elias joined them. He understood that it had been Madge Peary who had covered him with the blanket.

"How badly hurt are you?" she asked. "Can you walk?"

He waggled his head back and forth and felt his arms and legs. "I seem to still be all stuck in one piece," he said hoarsely.

His legs and body had been scraped by barnacles. His trousers were in tatters and his bare feet had taken punishment.

"You're bleeding," she said. She bent close and inspected his injuries. "They don't look too serious," she said. "I'll find some medicine and bandages. That'll help."

The golden girl turned and gazed scornfully at Strapp and Biggle. "Scoundrels!" she said. "You are cowards."

Strapp and some of the crew stood eying Webb. They were expecting him to show some sign of weakening. Of caving in. Waiting for him to crawl.

What they got was something else. "You should have left me down there, Strapp," he said.

"I'll do that the next time," Strapp said. But he had lost some of his sureness. There was an uneasiness in him.

Sidney Raines laughed. "I warned you that you were cutting a piece of cake that might be hard to chew, Jed," he said mockingly.

"I got mighty good teeth," Strapp snapped.

"Today you have," Elias growled. "Another day, you might find 'em missin'."

Strapp turned suddenly and walked away. The ship was rolling heavily. Spray was exploding over the foredeck. The wind heeled the vessel well over and whistled in the rigging.

Strapp bawled orders to shorten sail. Men swarmed into the rigging.

Elias and Webb shook hands, their clasp strong and thankful. "Figgered you was dead meat for sure that time, boy," Elias said. He coughed, trying to disprove that the thickness in his voice was emotion.

They made their way to the hold. No attempt was made to stop them. It was evident the crew had problems, for the wind seemed to be increasing in strength.

Elias returned above, and came back after a time with liniment and salve to doctor Webb's cuts and bruises, and with a pair of seamen's breeches that fitted fairly well. He had recovered Webb's poncho and other clothing that had been stripped from him before the keelhauling.

Elias went above again and returned, after a time, with plates of food and mugs of hot tea. The food was a stew of rice and salt pork that tasted delicious to their starved tongues. "The cook didn't take kindly to feedin' stowaways," Elias said. "But he changed his mind after I asked him how he'd look if he found his head set backwards on his shoulders."

"Why did they turn us loose?" Webb asked.

"Right now Strapp's got other worries, what with a stiff wind workin' up an' a lee shore to worry about in a ship that likely ain't none too frisky at standin' ag'in the breeze. Then, too, the Peary gal said somethin' to Strapp that took some o' the wind out of his sails."

"Why is she going out of her way to help a pair of strangers?" Webb speculated.

"Maybe she figures havin' strangers on her side is better'n no help at all."

"You could be right," Webb said. "We've got to have a talk with her."

"Maybe you better tell her where that poke is hid now," Elias said uneasily.

"It might be better if she didn't know," Webb said. "Sometimes knowledge can be a mighty painful thing."

"You mean they'd try to make her tell?"

"That's exactly what I mean and you know it as well as I do."

They climbed to the deck. The *Goodhaven* was running under shortened sails and safety lines had been stretched. They worked their way along the slanted deck to the cabin Madge Peary occupied. Webb knocked on the door.

"Who is it?" she demanded.

She had barricaded the door. After he had identified himself, he heard heavy objects, evidently trunks, being dragged aside. She opened the door, motioned them in and closed it quickly, wedging a bench against it.

She had her derringer in her hand, but replaced

it in her waist. The golden girl had been clutching a big cap-and-ball pistol with both hands. It was a handsome Paterson Colt with an elaborately carved barrel and an ivory handle. She laid the weapon on one of the berths, evidently thankful to be relieved of its weight.

The cabin was so small they were at close quarters, particularly after Elias had wedged himself into the place.

Webb looked at the pistol on the berth. "You seem to expect trouble," he said.

Madge Peary shrugged. "Has there been anything else lately?"

"Would this particular trouble be on account of having helped Elias and myself?"

"There could be other reasons," she said.

"Do you want to tell us about them?"

She debated it a moment with herself. "No," she said.

"At any rate we're mighty obliged to you," Webb said. "Whatever you used to persuade Strapp to turn us loose was mighty big medicine."

She smiled and still offered no explanation.

Webb turned to the other girl and said, "Once more I say *gracias, señorita. Muchas gracias!*"

"*¿Habla usted espanol?*" she exclaimed, bursting into a radiant smile. "You speak the Spanish?"

"Only a few words, I'm sorry to say," Webb explained. "Then you *are* Spanish?"

"My father, he was Spanish, yes."

95

"This is my sister," Madge Peary said. "The Princess Loa Martinique."

"Sister?" Webb echoed blankly. "Princess?"

Madge laughed. "Sister by adoption and affection. Princess by birth."

Webb stared. "Shouldn't you be wearing some sort of a golden crown, Princess? Where did you leave it?"

Loa Martinique laughed. "In a place of which you may never have heard. It is called Surabaya. And I am not a princess, no. My sister say that to make the fun."

"Her mother was a princess," Madge Peary said. "But they exiled her from the royal court when she married Loa's father. He was Juan Martinique, a Spanish gentleman and a sea captain from Manila in the Philippine Islands. He and my father were partners in the China trade for many years. Loa and I were born in the same house in Surabaya only two weeks apart. Our mothers were close friends. As babies, we sailed with our parents on voyages. I lived at her home in Surabaya as a child. She is the only sister I have, the only person alive who is very close to me. I love her very much."

"Surabaya," Webb said. "That would be on the island of Java, I believe. Then your mother, Miss Martinique, was Javanese?"

"That is so," Loa Martinique nodded, beaming. "You have been to Java, yes?"

"No," Webb said, smiling. "But it isn't as unknown as you seem to think."

"You have the education, Lieutenant Jernegan?"

Webb laughed and became aware of how painful were his puffed lips and bruised jaws. "Not yet," he said. "I'm still learning. Every day. I took one new lesson today. It was kind of you to remember my name."

"You mentioned it to us the other night in the store of this man we call Señor Stevens, and my sister told me all—"

Madge Peary abruptly interrupted her, obviously cutting off something she didn't want uttered. "We haven't the pleasure of knowing your name," she said, addressing Elias.

"Barnes, miss," Elias said, flustered. "Elias Barnes." He touched his forelock again. Reddening, he gave Webb a sidewise glance of apology.

"You talk like a Bedford man," Madge Peary said.

"That I am, miss. Or was. Born there."

"But you're not a seaman?"

"No, miss. I quit the sea as a lad. Sailed before the mast when I was fourteen. Two years on a whaler. When I set foot on land ag'in, I headed west. Headed for open country. I never wanted to smell salt water ag'in, or feel a deck under my feet. Never stopped goin' 'til I got to beaver country."

"What is this place, this beaver country?" Loa Martinique asked, puzzled.

"God's country, señorita. Mountains where there's big trees an' green meadows. Flowers in summer, with the birds whistlin'. A snug lodge to keep you warm, come winter, an' fat beaver tail in the pot. Deer an' elk yarded up in the meadows to feed. Runnin' streams when the ice breaks up in spring with trout jumpin' when you drop a line. Buffalo on the prairie. Fleece to roast over a fire, an' hump ribs sizzlin'."

Loa Martinique circled Elias in the cramped cabin, gazing in wide-eyed wonder, much to his embarrassment. "*Mira*! *Mira*!" she gushed. "How big you are! Like the big, big grizzly bear I have heard about in your mountains. How could one so huge make such beautiful talk about this place that he must love very much? You are one poet, Señor Elias Barnes. I wish to have you tell me more about this wonderful place."

"Some other time, Loa, dear," Madge said. She turned to Webb. "I doubt if you're as free as you believe. It's only that Strapp is busy handling the ship. This wind is working up into a gale. He'll get around to you again when he has time, I'm afraid."

Webb again eyed the pistol Loa had laid on the berth. "They took our guns," he said. "But Patersons like that usually come in pairs. If you could spare one . . . ?"

Madge thought it over for a moment. She turned

to Loa for advice and was given a nod of assent. Moving to a trunk, she produced a mate to the Paterson. It was loaded and capped. Webb placed it in his belt out of sight under the poncho.

"You seem to place a lot of confidence in us," he said. "Why?"

"Let's say that we need any friends we can find," she said. "We're not exactly happy with our situation on this ship."

"Raines?"

"We're not sure. Should we be as afraid of him as we are of Strapp?"

"Why be afraid of Strapp? You said this ship was yours. You must have hired him as captain."

"Hiring him was a matter of necessity. Men who could navigate ships weren't exactly plentiful in the part of the world from which we started this voyage in the *Goodhaven*. We knew his reputation, but we thought we could handle him. And we probably could have until this other man found out about—"

She broke off, as though realizing that she was getting into awkward ground also.

Webb finished it for her. "About that pouch of pretty stones that you hid in the paint locker?"

She and Loa Martinique stared at him, dumfounded.

"That pouch is no longer where you hid it," Webb said. That hit them hard. He saw vast despair in them. "I moved it to another hiding place," he said. "One that only Elias and I know about."

Anger came in them. And disillusionment and resentment. "You intend to keep them, of course," Madge said bitterly.

"I'm not sure," Webb said.

"Not sure? What do you mean, you're not sure?"

"I've got a hunch you'd be better off if you didn't know what we did with that pouch. What you don't know, you can't tell. Do you follow me?"

"I believe I do," she said. Her voice was suddenly hollow.

"Sid Raines is the kind of a man who won't be squeamish how he goes about getting money or anything worth money," Webb said. "Especially big money. Strapp is all bone and muscle. Easy to read, but hard to down in a fight. Raines is all of that, and with brains to boot. And no heart. He can fight. With guns or fists. He's one of the best shots with a rifle I've ever seen. But he prefers to shoot you in the back."

She shivered a little. She seemed to be debating something in her mind. "You came a long distance to find him, apparently," she said abruptly.

"Nearly two months by trail," Webb said. "From Taos. That's in New Mexico. We came by Fremont's route over the middle mountains, and Carson's way over the Sierra Nevada mountains."

"Then you could easily find your way back by the same route?"

Webb peered, suddenly realizing what this as leading to. "Yes, but there'd be nothing easy about it. You're no more than a meal away from starvation or a swallow away from dying of thirst on long stretches of that trail. And that's not to mention the Indians. You never know what they might take a notion to do."

"If Loa and I decide to go east overland, will you two guide us?"

"Hold on! You don't know what it's like. It's rough enough on a man. But a woman—"

"Anything might be better than staying on this ship. And I believe that goes for you also, and Mr. Barnes, if what you say about Raines is true. None of us might live to see land again."

"But you own this ship. Do you mean to abandon it?"

"Better that than having it as a coffin."

"How would we get ashore?"

"There's only one way. Seize the ship's boat. We'd have to wait for the right chance."

"If I leave," Webb said, "Raines goes with me. All the way."

"Is that necessary?"

"Very necessary."

"I agree, provided the pouch of stones also goes with us, in the possession of Loa or myself, of course."

"That brings up a matter that I'm curious about," Webb said. "Elias said he believed you told Jed Strapp something that caused him to back off of any more tricks like keelhauling us. That was the big medicine I mentioned a while ago. I've got a hunch I can guess how that medicine was brewed."

She only shrugged and did not answer.

"It was the pretty stones, wasn't it?" Webb persisted. "What did you say to him?"

"I told him I'd throw them overboard if murder was committed on this ship," she said levelly.

"And would you have done it?"

She smiled a little, mockingly. "You'll never know. I don't know that answer myself."

"Do you want to tell us how much those pretty little pebbles are worth?" Webb asked. He added, "You don't have to, of course. It won't change things, either way."

"Upward of a quarter of a million, I believe," she said calmly. "Perhaps twice that much after they're polished by experts."

Webb whistled. "A nice, tidy sum to split up."

Her cool smile did not change. "If you have any idea of declaring yourself in on any split, you're in for a big disappointment. There'll be no sharing of the proceeds from the stones. At least among the four of us."

She added. "The fact is the pretty stones aren't ours to share."

"Not yours!" Webb exclaimed. "Whose are they?"

Before she could answer, a fist hammered the door. "What's goin' on in there?" Biggle yelled in shrill voice. "The cap'n says fer ye two to come out on deck."

"Strapp's found time to remember you," Madge said. "Maybe the effect of the big medicine has left him."

"We'll talk this over in the morning," Webb said.

"By morning we'll be too far at sea, most likely, to try to make it to shore in a small-boat."

"Lady," Elias said, "we ain't afeard o' Raines. An' Strapp, least o' all. We won't let you get hurt. Keep that in mind."

She smiled wanly. "I'm sure you won't—if you're around."

Webb patted the pistol under his poncho. "We'll be around," he promised.

He opened the door and he and Elias stepped out. Biggle and two seamen were awaiting them, armed with shotguns and pistols. In the background stood Strapp and Raines, also with pistols in their hands.

"The cap'n says fer me to put ye below decks 'til he gits time to figger out what to do with ye," Biggle said.

Elias uttered a rumble of opposition, but Webb said quickly, "No! That's what they want—an excuse to shoot us down."

Biggle prodded them down a dark companion-way and through a narrow door, which was slammed back of them and bolted. They found themselves in a dank, confined space as cold as a tomb and alive with the groaning and creaking of the ship and the slamming of the waves.

"Eye of the ship," Elias said. "Hell's last berth."

The sea seemed to be with them. It pounded at the planks beside them. It was a monster, snarling and gnawing, trying to get at them. Webb felt his stomach begin to spin. This cell was the creation of a nightmare. It was like trying to remain sane on the back of a pitching mustang.

The blanket Madge Peary had given them was their salvation. Both he and Elias warmed at last and fell into troubled sleep.

Whenever Webb aroused, it seemed to him that the groaning and working of the ship was more agonized.

Once he heard Elias start up and mumble, "This craft's in bad trouble!"

Chapter Seven

Webb judged that it was midmorning when he finally awakened completely. He could only guess at the time, for there was no way of telling daybreak from dusk in their gloomy prison.

He was rested, but he was hungry. He was stiff and aching. He knew he must be a sorry sight, with his bruised, blood-crusted features, unshaven and gaunted by the ordeal of the past hours.

The gale apparently was blowing harder than before and the ship was making hard weather of it. At times the vessel would roll far on her beam ends and lie in that position for so long Webb felt it impossible she would ever right herself again. But she always managed to recover sluggishly, only to be pounced on again by wind and sea. Then the battle would repeat itself.

"This is what comes o' runnin' light in ballast," Elias said gloomily. "I told you what'd happen if we run into a blow aboard this tub."

"You told me," Webb agreed.

They tested the door. It gave a trifle when they both put their weight against it. They let it go at that, deciding they would be able to escape if they made a real effort, but that it would be better to keep that knowledge to themselves for the present.

That lessened the fear of being trapped and going down with the *Goodhaven* if worst came to worst. They would at least have a chance for their lives.

They sat in silence, waiting. The ship's travail went on, hour after hour. They became so hardened to the danger and strain they made a grim game of it, wagering imaginary huge sums on the length of time the vessel required to recover from its batterings in the troughs of the waves.

It was late afternoon, Webb judged, when a crash and terrified shouting on deck brought them to their feet.

Elias clung to beams while the ship rolled sickeningly. "Sounds like a mast went that time," he said.

"Then it's also time for us to get out of this rat hole!" Webb exclaimed.

They rammed the door with their shoulders and felt the bolt's moorings give a trifle. They backed away and charged again. This time they burst free.

Reaching the deck, they crouched, clinging to the life line. Around them, the sea was a wind-beaten wilderness. The *Goodhaven* seemed pitifully puny on the face of this waste of wild waves.

Elias pointed upward. Webb saw a tangle of shrouds and torn sails. A mast had broken.

His gaze swung in another direction. "Look!" he shouted above the roar of the wind.

Looming out of the flying spray and foam, scarcely two miles away, was an ominous gray-green mass.

Land! The coast! Somber, brush-clad mountains rose from the white boil where the surf raged at the base of rocky bluffs.

"Lee shore!" Elias shouted. "This ship's done for. We'll be on the rocks inside half an hour."

Biggle and a husky seaman, both with double-barreled shotguns in their hands and braces of pistols strapped outside their oilskins, stood on the afterdeck guarding the ship's small-boat, which had been freed of its canvas and was slung overside from davits. Webb saw that the boat was heavily provisioned with tins of biscuits and slabs of salt pork.

"They're gettin' ready to abandon ship," Elias said. He peered up and down the decks. "An' that's the only boat aboard. There was two more lifeboats at one time, but their davits are empty. They must have been lost long ago."

The lone small-boat, Webb saw, would accommodate no more than half a dozen persons. The remaining members of the crew were crouched in the lee of a deckhouse. There were seven of them. They were gazing numbly at the shore toward which the ship was being driven. The helm had been abandoned. The wheel spun wildly as the ship was driven at the mercy of the wind and the sea.

Webb went racing to the cabin occupied by the girls and pounded on the door. It was jerked open. Elias had followed him, and they stared, startled, into the muzzles of pistols. The weapons were in the hands of Jed Strapp. Beyond him Webb saw Sid Raines in the cabin with the girls. Both Raines and Strapp were wearing oilskins.

"Stand back, you two!" Strapp barked. "This is none of your affair."

Madge and Loa Martinique, white-faced, also were pulling on oilskins. Loa had abandoned her exotic garb in favor of a sea jacket and occidental skirt and petticoats. Their trunks stood open, with clothing scattered about. They clutched small bundles that evidently contained what possessions they were able to carry.

"Are you sure you've got *all* your valuables?" Raines was asking. He attempted to take the bundle Madge clutched, but she refused to surrender it and backed away from him.

In spite of her pallor, there was mockery in her voice as she said, "Now what valuables would we have?"

Strapp whirled on her, his face savage. "Don't try any of your snooty talk with us, blast you! You know what we mean!"

"Yes," she said. "I know what you mean."

She pushed past them and stepped on deck,

drawing Loa with her. At close range she gave Webb a quick glance and a wan smile. "You were right," she murmured.

No other word was spoken by them, but Webb knew what she meant. She was telling him that he had been right in keeping from her the knowledge of the new hiding place of the pouch.

Raines came striding, overtook her, caught her roughly by the arm and hurried her down the deck. Strapp followed clutching Loa's arm, almost carrying her bodily toward the waiting lifeboat. Strapp tossed the two girls into the boat. Webb saw Raines wrest the bundle from Madge's grasp. He kept it clutched in his arm, but tossed into the bottom of the boat the satchel of valuables he had salvaged from his burning trading post. He and Strapp leaped into the boat.

Elias was fuming, but Webb stood grimly watching. Any attempt to interfere would be certain to start a gun fight in which the two girls would be in the line of fire. The chances were they would be used as shields.

A moaning sound arose from the crew. The men aroused from their apathy, suddenly realizing that the captain was leaving them to shift for themselves. Screams and curses arose. They started to charge the boat.

Biggle, who was helping the seaman lower the boat, lifted his shotgun and fired one barrel. The heavy charge killed a sailor, the buckshot nearly breaking the man in two. Blood drained off into the scuppers, washed away by the next wave that swept the deck.

That halted the others. They retreated to the shelter of the deckhouse and crouched there, watching dully as the boat was lowered. Biggle and the seaman slid down the lines and cast off.

For a moment the small craft was in danger of being smashed against the ship's side. Then waves carried it clear. Oars were in motion and the boat began fighting its way southward. Webb saw a promontory in that direction and guessed that if the craft rounded it, there might be calmer water in its lee.

He and Elias made their way to the paint locker. The chamois pouch was still intact in the crevice where Webb had hidden it.

"One man dead already on account o' them things," Elias said. "This ship would never have made this voyage but for them purty stones. Who's goin' to be the next to go? Maybe you, or me."

They returned to the deck. Elias, being a practical man, appraised the situation and said, "We've got time to see if we can't raise a bait o' grub. We'll need it, you hear me now, if we're to have the strength to land on that rocky lee shore."

He led the way to the galley. The remains of the last meal were in a pot that swung over the galley stove. They ate this in a hurry, and downed a mug of lukewarm tea.

Going back on deck they gazed at the shore. The thunder of the surf was like muffled cannon fire. They were so close they could see foam and spray being tossed high against the foot of the bluffs.

The men of the crew emerged from their apathy of terror and were making a belated attempt to abandon the ship. They had removed the heavy plank cover from the hatch and had slid it overboard to serve as a raft.

"You'll be better off staying with the ship until she strikes," Webb warned them.

They didn't listen to him. They were too terrified. Equipping themselves with improvised oars and paddles, they frantically leaped from the rail onto the hatch. It was swept clear of the lee of the ship into the boil of waves.

A savage wall of hissing green water buried hatch and men in the next instant. Only four men were still clinging to the improvised raft when it surfaced again. A second wave buried it. All that Webb and Elias could see after that were the heads of two men who managed to stay afloat for a time.

One of these, a strong swimmer, made it as far as the thundering surf that battered the rocks. That was all. He vanished and never reappeared in that millrace of foam.

The boat carrying the other six survivors was visible, rounding the promontory to the south.

"Looks like they're a-goin' to make it, if they can find a decent place to run ashore," Elias said.

Around them, rats were scurrying on the slanting deck, driven from the hold by rising water, for sea poured into the hold through the open hatch with each raking comber. The *Goodhaven* was down by the head and lying partly on her port side. Just ahead, spray was spurting like powder explosions on a reef a hundred yards from the shore proper.

The *Goodhaven* struck hard on the reef and the last of the wrecked shrouds and rigging crashed overboard. Webb and Elias nearly accompanied it as green water buried the vessel and them with it.

The ship clung on the reef for a moment while Webb and Elias desperately grasped the stub of a foremast that was above-water.

Webb felt the ship being lifted clear by the next comber. She surged sluggishly toward the shore and struck again amid the wild surf at the base of the bluffs.

This brought her around broadside and, miraculously, she rolled almost upright. A wave drove her higher onto the rocks. The next wave swept entirely over her. Webb and Elias realized that this was their chance.

They let the wave carry them clear and toward

the base of the bluffs. The ship had acted as a bulwark, tempering the full fury of the comber, and though it was breaking up, it still offered a lee and that gave them a chance for their lives.

Webb let himself go limp as the sea swept him toward the rocks. He was dashed against something solid with a dazing impact. He was swirled this way and that in a turmoil of boiling water and collided with more unyielding objects.

The wave started to recede and to carry him back into the trough of the next comber that would finish him. But he managed to wrap his arms around a boulder around which a mass of seaweed had lodged. He hung on as the water receded.

He found himself on firm land with the drain from the receding comber racing around his ankles. He staggered up the slant toward the base of the bluff. Elias was at his side, also fighting to escape before the next wave dragged them back.

The wave came and clutched them around the waist, seeking to hold them, but they fought it off and it receded. They managed to scramble up the face of the bluff, which was not as abrupt as Webb had feared. It offered foot- and hand-holds.

They reached a resting place above the reach of the waves and spray and stayed there for a long time, exhausted. Finally, they managed to work their way higher. And higher.

Webb realized that darkness was coming. They fought their way to a break in the face of the bluff where a landslip in the past had created a step wide enough on which to throw themselves prone and lie until life sluggishly revived.

By that time full darkness had come. A few faint stars were showing through the mist in a gale-swept sky. Elias spoke, his voice a croak, "The sea's only for the dead. I never want to see it ag'in, you hear me now?"

"Look, there along that beach below us to the south," Webb said. "That's no star. It's on land."

A distant faint dot of red stood out in the darkness. It was a fire.

"They made it," Webb said. "It must be them. They'd have dry matches, or flint and steel and gunpowder to start a fire."

He reached inside his soaked shirt. "I've still got the bag of pretty stones," he said, dully surprised. "I'd forgotten it." He added, wearily, "But my gun's gone."

"So's mine," Elias said. "Got rid of it in the water when I was close to drownin'. They'd be no good to us anyway, with powder wet an' nothing with which to reprime."

Webb got to his feet. "We could use some of that fire," he said. "This wind cuts right to the quick."

"But they'll have powder for their guns," Elias warned.

Webb hefted the wet pouch of gems in the

soaked chamois. "This medicine was strong once before. Maybe it's still stronger than gunpowder," he said.

Leading the way, he found that the path formed by the lip of the landslip led to a break in the face of the bluff. They worked their way along a brushy slope and that brought them out on an open, rounded hillside, fairly free of chaparral, from which they had a better view southward.

The fire they had sighted was a bright, red eye in the darkness of a sizable cove, which had a flat, rocky beach against which surf broke whitely. Descending to more level ground, they could see figures silhouetted against the blaze, which seemed elevated slightly above the surroundings. Two of these figures wore skirts.

Webb's teeth were chattering and he was beginning to shiver uncontrollably. Elias was in the same predicament. The wind was biting through their soaked garb like the icy breath of death itself.

They worked their way nearer the fire. They could smell its smoke. Once, the wind changed and they even felt its faint warmth. Webb drew a deeper sigh. Then the wind changed and its chill knifed through them again.

"If this was Ute or Pawnee country, their scalps would be stretched on a frame in a lodge, come daybreak," Elias chattered. "Look at the size o' that blaze."

But there were no Utes on this bleak coast. Nor Pawnees. And there likely was little to fear from the fish-eating coastal tribes if any happened to be in this region.

The fire, built of driftwood, was roaring, casting its glow farther over the beach as fuel was added with a prodigal hand. Webb could see the cast-aways huddling close to the warmth. The ship's boat lay abandoned and capsized in the surf, where waves battered it against the rocks that studded the sand.

The beach consisted mainly of a riprap of small, rounded rocks that were at the mercy of the ceaseless rush of the surf. When each wave fell back, small, moving, loose rocks lifted a hollow, ghostly, rattling chorus, an eerie sound in the darkness.

Crawling on hands and knees and taking advantage of the contour of land and of boulders and patches of stiff, low brush, Webb and Elias moved in. They finally flattened out, little more than a hundred feet from the camp.

The fire had been built on a flat table of rock a hundred or more feet in length and irregularly half that in width, which stood half a dozen feet above the beach proper. The seaward side of this refuge stood almost in the surf, with the heavier waves rushing to surge around its base. It was here that the rolling stones lifted the ghostly refrain the loudest.

Webb peered cautiously. Madge Peary and Loa Martinique seemed to be unharmed. They sat together within reach of the fire's warmth. They had removed the oilskins and their sea jackets, which were propped on driftwood to dry. Their dresses, which were wet and clinging to their bodies, were steaming in the warmth.

Raines and Strapp, along with Biggle and the seaman, had stripped to the waist and were drying their garments also, moving around the fire as the wind changed, driving heat and smoke upon them.

Evidently the boat had capsized and they all had been pitched into the surf but had reached the beach. The bulk of the provisions apparently had been cast ashore and salvaged, for tins of biscuits and kegs of salt pork stood near the fire.

Webb remembered the satchel Raines had tossed in the boat. It was not in sight and he realized it must have been lost in the capsizing, weighted down by the coin Raines had salvaged from the safe in his burning store at Yerba Buena.

"Maybe their powder's wet too!" Elias breathed.

That hope faded. As though spurred by the same thought, Raines at that moment finished reloading a six-shooter he had dried by the fire. He pointed the muzzle into the sky and pulled the trigger. The pistol fired.

Startled, Madge and Loa screamed wildly.

Raines smiled. Webb realized that he had

intended to frighten them. "I only wanted to make sure the gun was in good shape, ladies," Raines said. "I wasn't aiming at anybody." He added, "At least, not yet."

The bundles of spare clothing belonging to the two girls had been torn open and the garments were scattered around. Evidently Raines and Strapp had searched for the pouch of gems.

Madge and Loa sat looking up at Raines. Suddenly, they leaped to their feet and attempted to run. They meant to jump to the beach and try to escape into the darkness.

Raines overtook and seized Madge, whirling her and sending her to her knees. She had drawn the derringer, but he gripped her wrist, forcing the muzzle into the air, compelling her to press the trigger. The hammer clicked emptily. The priming was wet.

At the same time, Loa had been seized by Strapp. He clamped an arm around her, holding her helpless. "Just look at what this one had," he said, grinning. "One o' them cussed crooked Malay knives. You might have had it in your hide, mister, except for me."

Elias nudged Webb and murmured, "I told you so."

For Loa, with a gasp of pain, was forced to drop a small, silver-handled dagger with a sinuous blade as Strapp applied pressure. A kris.

"That's no plaything for a gal to carry around,"

Strapp said. "Don't you ever try to use it on us ag'in."

"*Perro!*" Loa spat. "*Lechon*! Dog! Pig. Take your filthy hands off me!"

The two girls were brought back to the fire and pushed roughly to the ground. Raines stood over them, looking down at them. There was no particular emotion in his face. It was as though he was judging them as he would judge some refractory animal. He seemed completely impersonal. Yet, Webb felt that he had never seen such hard purpose in a man's eyes. In the background, Biggle and the seaman were on their feet, staring uneasily. In them was some of the same horror that Webb felt.

"I'll take charge of those items you have on you, my dear," he said to Madge.

"What do you mean?"

"You know what I mean. The items your father stole from that Malay village."

"I haven't got them," she said.

"Do you want us to strip your clothes from you to find them?"

"I didn't have them when I left the ship," she said.

Raines seized her by the hair and shook her. She still had the derringer. She tried to use it as a club, for its priming evidently was useless. Raines warded off the blow with ease. She gave it up as hopeless and returned the weapon to her waist.

Raines shook her brutally again, then stepped back. Her hair tumbled down over her shoulders. "Be easy on yourself," he said. "You know you'll have to hand them over sooner or later."

"They may have gone down with the *Good-haven*," she said.

There was a moment of silence. "What do you mean, they *may* have gone down with the *Goodhaven*?" Raines asked. His voice was still quiet, but now he was ashen, and there was cold fury in him.

"I hid them in the paint locker when I came aboard that night at Yerba Buena," she said. "But someone—"

"Why did you hide them?"

She gazed up at him exhaustedly. "I'm sure you know why. You had found out there were more pearls when I made the mistake of agreeing to pay you off with two of them. You probably wrung the truth out of Strapp and both of you went into cahoots to get them away from me."

She added, "Someone else saw me hide them. He's the one who has them. That's the truth."

Again there was silence. Madge turned, looking at Strapp.

"So it was you, Jed?" Raines growled.

Strapp's voice rose to an injured squeak. "Me? She's a-lyin'! I never—"

"Have you got them, Jed?" Raines demanded.

"Don't let her make a fool of you, man," Strapp

raged. "She's only tryin' to get us to clawin' at each other. I never was in that paint locker."

Raines studied Strapp for a space and seemed to decide he was telling the truth. He smiled at Madge. "You are a very intelligent person," he said. "That I admire. The first thing the tactical handbook taught me in the Army was that a divided opponent was much easier to defeat."

"Then you *were* an Army officer?" she said. "Your real name is Sidney Raines and not Frank Stevens. You admit it, don't you?"

"Apparently you've had a considerable conversation with Webb Jernegan."

She didn't answer that. Raines again caught her by the hair, starting to shake her. She kicked and scratched desperately, trying to break free.

Raines had his hands full for a time, but he finally overpowered her. Her strength gave out, although she kept feebly trying to struggle.

"All right," Raines said. "Now tell the truth. Exactly where are they?"

"I've told you," she gasped. "The pouch was gone. Someone had taken it from where I had hidden it."

Raines spoke to Strapp. "Miss Martinique seems to be a little chilly. Perhaps she needs to be warmed. Closer to the fire might do it, Captain."

Strapp hesitated, his fish-belly face a study. With all his reputation for brutality, he did not like this.

"A quarter of a million dollars, Captain," Raines said mockingly. "Maybe double that much. You said so yourself. Think of what you could do with money like that."

Strapp said huskily, "You devil!" He suddenly seized Loa and pulled her to her feet. "You're pretty," he said. "Prettier'n any woman I ever had this close before."

"And I will never be clean again," Loa panted. "You are vile. You are one low animal. But even you are not as low as that other one."

"Hear that, Jed?" Raines said. "She despises you. Maybe she might change her mind with a little persuasion."

Strapp lifted her clear of the ground, held her like a doll in his extended arms. "I'm the one what can do just that," he said. "You treated me like dirt under your slippers all the way from the China Sea. Now you'll sing another song."

He moved nearer the flames, holding her in front of him to shield his own body from the heat, but exposing her to the full impact of the fire whose heart was now white-hot.

Loa uttered no sound, although even at the first moment she must have felt the savage touch of the flames.

Madge uttered a scream. "Not her! Not my sister! Don't harm her! She knows nothing about the stones."

"But you do?" Raines snapped.

"Yes. I've told you all I know."

Raines spoke to Strapp. "A little closer. Brown her a little. She's a trifle too golden in color. She needs a little basting."

Madge went to her knees. "I swear I've told you the truth," she sobbed. "Don't torture Loa! She can't help you!"

Webb moved. He ran crouched in the darkness and reached the outcrop of the rock table on the seaward side. The tide was flooding in. Each incoming wave raced higher on the beach, slapping the base of the flat expanse where the fire blazed.

A wave swirled around Webb's knees as he worked his way along the face of the outcrop. As it receded, the eerie clacking of the rounded stones arose around him.

The outcrop stood some ten feet above the tide line at this point, but he found footholds and mounted.

They did not see him at first as he appeared in the firelight. They were all staring at Strapp and Loa. Of them all, Loa seemed the most composed. Strapp had edged nearer the fire, still using her as his shield, his arm clamped around her waist.

Webb doubted if she had been actually injured as yet by the heat, but if she was held in that position much longer she would soon be in agony. She was struggling with grim and lithe determination. She was not giving in to hysteria.

There was proud rage in her. A noble fury. She would never break or beg for mercy. Nor was she submitting meekly. She fought with silent and ceaseless intensity.

Even Strapp's strength was being tested. "You devil-cat!" he panted. "D'you want me to break you right in two? Quit squirmin'!"

But she didn't quit. Biggle and the seaman had backed still farther away. Raines stood holding Madge helpless as she struggled to help Loa.

"Please!" Madge kept gasping. "Please! If you have to torture someone, I'm the one who—!"

"Do not beg, *querida mia*," Loa said. "They are not men. They are demons."

Webb spoke. "Is this what you're so bent on getting your hands on, Sid?"

Their heads jerked around as though moved by the same string. They gaped incredulously. Strapp's grasp released for an instant so that Loa, with a convulsive burst of lithe strength, broke away from him. She snatched up the kris from where it had fallen.

"Now!" she panted. "It is my turn!"

She could have plunged the dagger into Strapp's chest. Instead, in a supreme gesture of contempt for him, she brandished the wicked blade before his face, flickering it back and forth in mocking, lightning strokes that seemed to graze his nose.

Strapp recoiled in a panic. She kept him in

retreat, following him like an angry terrier. Before he could recover his balance she gave him a mighty push. Strapp sprawled backward. He escaped plunging into the main fire, but a hand that he thrust out to break his fall found hot ashes and embers. He uttered a yelp of pain.

Loa raced to Webb's side and crouched close to him. She now began to weep hysterically.

Her escape and Strapp's discomfiture had happened with such speed that there had been no opportunity for Raines to intervene. Strapp rolled clear of the fire, beating at sparks on his clothes. He began to curse frenziedly.

Raines released Madge and lifted his pistol. He intended to shoot Webb.

"Hold it, Sid," Webb said. "A bullet would knock me right off this rock into that incoming tide. All these pretty little stones in this bag would get spilled down there. I don't imagine any of them would ever be found again, what with all those rocks rolling around and the waves never quitting."

Webb held in his hands the pouch of gems. He worked at the wet drawstring, handling the soaked chamois gingerly. He poured a few of the jewels into the palm of his hand, then let them drop back into the pouch.

"You see," he said, "someone did move them from the place Miss Peary had hidden them in the paint locker. Me! She was telling you the truth."

Raines did not fire. He stood gazing, his mind weighing the situation.

Madge leaped to her feet, meaning to race to join Webb and Loa, but Raines caught her by the arm with his left hand and held her beside him. "Stand still!" he said.

"Eli and I holed up in the paint locker when we first came aboard," Webb said. "We saw her hide the pouch and I helped myself to it after she had left."

"And so . . . ?" Raines inquired.

"There's no longer any point in trying to bluff that you'd torture Miss Martinique until Miss Peary talked," Webb said.

"I wasn't bluffing," Raines said.

"No," Webb said. "I'm afraid you weren't."

"What's on your mind?" Raines demanded.

Webb considered. "First, let Miss Peary come over here with me. The rest of you back off. Far enough so that I can keep an eye on you but don't have to worry about you."

Raines laughed grimly. "Look who's giving orders. You seem to be looking at things upside down. I'll call the tune. You dance."

Webb again dribbled some of the precious stones from the pouch into his hand and back. "Do you suppose these things are really worth a quarter of a million, Sid?" he asked.

"You tell me," Raines said.

"Things are worth what you can get for them at

the time," Webb said. "Depends on circumstances. There've been times in the last three years when I'd have given plenty for a square meal. Or a roof over my head. I'd have given a lot more than a quarter of a million, if I'd had it, to have got my hands on you. I'd have sold my soul to the devil. Fact is, maybe I've done just that. Eli thinks so. At least it was worth it. For I've found you at last."

"You're still looking through the wrong end of the glass," Raines said. "It seems that *I've* found you."

"As I said before," Webb declared, "that depends on the circumstances. We want a rifle and two pistols. And that powder pouch and the cap-and-ball pouch that Strapp's carrying. And the knife in Biggle's belt. Flint and steel. Also a good share of the grub you have. Enough to carry us a few days."

"Shoot him!" Strapp exploded. "Quit wastin' time. He's talkin' crazy."

Raines said icily, "Shut up! I'll do the talking—and the deciding when to shoot."

"You don't think I'm goin' to stand for—!" Strapp began, outraged.

He broke off with a gurgle of consternation. Webb had lifted one of the gems—a pearl. Poising it between his forefinger and thumb, he aimed it toward the outer darkness.

"I would say that I'm calling the tune," he said.

He flipped the pearl away. It formed a small brilliant arc of reflected firelight, then dropped into the darkness, falling to the sea-washed, rocky beach.

"If you want to try to find that one," he said, "we'll wait. There's no hurry."

Raines stiffened and looked a trifle ill.

Webb laughed. "That hit you right where you live, didn't it Sid. That was like taking it right out of your pocket. You never were one to be a good loser."

Strapp broke again into frenzied profanity. Loa had uttered a sigh of regret at the loss of the stone. But it was Madge's reaction that held Webb's gaze. She was looking at him with an approval that was wild and almost gleeful, as though he had performed a feat that she envied.

Strapp lifted his pistol, cocking the hammer. "Toss me that poke, fella, or I'll put so much lead in you that—"

"Put down that gun, you idiot," Raines said harshly.

"He's the one that's bluffin'!" Strapp protested.

Raines shook his head. "Not this man. Put your cap pouch and canister on the rock. And that pistol. Biggle, you can add your knife to the collection, and then put some of the biscuits and meat—"

"I ain't lettin' him get away with this!" Strapp screeched.

"You'd be an easy mark in a poker game, Strapp," Webb said. "Didn't anyone ever tell you never to call a hand when you already know you're beaten?"

"As long as we can kill you, Webb," Raines said, "I hardly believe we hold the losing hand. However, of course, we expect some reward for furnishing you with the arms and provisions."

"I expected you would," Webb said.

"I imagine you know the terms," Raines said.

"I can guess," Webb said. He hefted the pouch. "I'll leave this on the rock. Handle it careful. Wet chamois will break if you get careless. These pretty stones are heavier than you'd believe until you lifted them."

He looked at Madge. "Is that satisfactory to you?"

"No," she said.

Webb eyed her. "You don't seem to care much about staying alive."

"I told you before that those stones aren't mine to give away. Or yours."

"You're a puzzle to me," Webb said. "But, for your own sake, I'll decide this." He nodded to Raines. "All right."

Strapp was silenced. Raines said, "How do we know you'll keep your part of the bargain?"

Webb considered that for a moment. He called to Elias to join him and the big man came scrambling out of the darkness to the surface of the rock and stood beside him.

"First," he said. "Eli will make sure you've kept your part of it. He'll come back here with the pistols and food. Then I'll move in and put the pouch in your reach. Eli will kill you at the first sign of a wrong move, Sid."

"It'd be a cryin' pleasure," Elias said.

"One more thing," Webb said. "The ladies go with us."

"Take them and be damned to them," Raines said.

Chapter Eight

The agreement was carried out on Webb's terms. The weapons and ammunition were placed near the fire, along with a grudging portion of the provisions.

Elias moved in, made sure the pistols were in working order and that the powder and lead were satisfactory. He thrust the pistols in his belt, gathered up the rifle and food and returned to the lip of the rock.

From that position he stood with the pistols, covering Strapp and Raines as Webb walked in and placed the pouch of stones on the rock. The instant Webb retreated, Raines pounced on the pouch. Opening it, he dribbled the contents through his fingers, examining the gems closely. He looked at Webb with a cynical smile of triumph.

Webb said, "There'll be another day, Sid. I'll find you again. Keep that in mind, always."

He and Elias swung the two girls down from the rock into the darkness of the beach. Leaping to join them, they retreated at a run, stumbling over boulders in the darkness and staggering through yielding sand.

The glow of the fire faded behind them and

finally Webb slowed the pace. "How about you?" he asked Loa. "Were you burned?"

"I am not hurt," she said. "You came in time."

She began to sob and wring her hands, stumbling blindly in the rough underfooting.

Elias took her arm, helping her along. "What's the use o' blubberin' now, after the way you stood up to 'em when it counted?"

"I cannot help it," she wailed. "It makes me feel much better, this crying. I want to cry. It makes me happy."

"Then keep it up," Elias said. "But I got to say, miss, it's a mighty queer way o' havin' a good time."

Webb led the way off the beach. They followed the bed of a dry creek, whose sandy bottom, gleaming faintly in the starlight, offered a visible pathway in contrast to the blackness of the surrounding brush.

This faded and they worked their way to the rim of a low ridge, which they followed farther away from the ocean. They were half-carrying the girls the greater part of the time.

Finally Webb found a small barranca, whose banks were high enough to shelter them from the wind. He gathered dry twigs. With flint and steel and a pinch of gunpowder he sparked a fire. He added fuel and they hovered close to the flames.

"Not long ago I feel that I never want to see fire

again or feel heat," Loa chattered. "Now, I thank the radiance of heaven for this."

Presently, Webb left the gully and scouted the brushy flank of the mountain. The gale still blew in from the sea, roaring over the crest of a ridge above him. He climbed to that crest—an effort of will, for he was nearing the limit of his physical endurance.

There, he faced the full force of the wind. But from that vantage point he could see the ocean and the cove where Strapp and Raines had built their fire. But the beach was black and formless—deserted. No fire blazed there. Strapp and Raines had left the rock.

On the other hand, their own fire in the barranca was not visible from above. In fact, it was so well hidden from observation in all directions that he almost missed it as he descended the slope.

When he finally walked into the camp, he found the two girls huddled together for warmth on a bed of dry leaves that Elias had gathered. Loa had fallen into exhausted sleep, but Madge was awake. Her eyes asked him a question.

"It's all right," he said. "There's not a chance in a hundred they could find us here, even if they tried."

She nodded. That was what had been on her mind. Reassured, she too fell asleep. Webb and Elias slept also. But, in spite of their weariness, they awakened often to refuel the fire, or to listen.

Webb was aware that Madge awakened often also and lay listening. She knew that, despite his assurance, there was always the chance that Raines and Strapp might discover their hiding place and be creeping through the darkness, seeking a chance to bushwhack them.

But it was always only the wind and its prowling through the chaparral that they heard.

The violence of the gale faded toward daybreak, but a cold wind still droned through the brush when Webb finally aroused. He and Elias suffered in silence as they struggled into boots and moccasins that had stiffened and shrunk from being dried beside the fire.

The girls awakened and sat forlorn and too beaten of spirit to even talk.

Webb chucked Loa under the chin. "We'll all feel better with a little grub to chaw on."

She attempted a wan smile. "What is this thing, this grub? This chaw?"

"*Kau kau*," Madge explained. "Food! Chaw means eating."

"*Si, si!*" Loa exclaimed, brightening. "I am very hungry. I will be happy with this grub and chaw."

"There's a small stream in a draw below here, from the looks of those green willows," Webb said. "Maybe we can find water to drink. We'll cook some of this salt horse. You all look like you could use a little water. Soap too, if we had any handy, which we haven't."

"Well, I can tell you that you're no tearin' beauty either, boy," Elias said. "You look more like you belong in a den o' loafer wolves than among human bein's."

Webb saw what Elias meant when he caught a glimpse of his reflection in a quiet pool in the creek, beside which they cooked skewered meat. Gazing back at him were eyes gray and wild set deep in a saddle-brown, unshaven face that was drawn and taut-lipped. He guessed that more pounds had been lost from his lank frame.

He stared, shocked. He discovered that Madge and Loa were watching him, amused by his consternation. Daylight, food and the activity of moving camp had given them a new lease on life.

They had bathed their faces at the stream. Madge began plaiting her hair in a long pigtail. Loa had managed, amazingly, to keep possession of her big Spanish shell comb with its glittering brilliants. She busied herself arranging her hair and finished off the effect by placing the comb to best advantage. This revived her buoyant spirit.

She spoke to Madge, but made sure Webb could hear. "That one surely cannot be the man you told me about," she said. "The one you say for whom they named the *niños*. Not that ragged *pelado*?"

"He's the one," Madge said. "The very one. Those poor babies."

Webb glared at them suspiciously. He knew he was being baited, but he was unable to guess what they were driving at. The reference to *niños*, or babies, was beyond him.

"At least it's nice to see that you two aren't worried any longer about hobgoblins in the dark," he said.

Madge became serious. "I'm afraid the hobgoblins won't bother to haunt us any longer. They've got what they want from us."

Webb doused his head in the stream. The shock of the cold water was electric, but it was also cleansing, revivifying. He leaned back, puffing and blowing, flirting water from his hair with his hands.

"Maybe I haven't got what I want from them," he said.

"You're not through with the hobgoblins, are you?" she asked slowly. "It's you who'll do the haunting."

"Yes," Webb said.

"You'll keep haunting Raines until either he or you is dead. That's it, isn't it?"

"Could be," Webb said.

"You told him that night in the store that you had been sentenced to hang for his murder."

"That's right."

"You seem to be cool enough about it," she said angrily.

Webb was surprised, puzzled by the way she

seemed offended with him. "I've lived with it too long to go around beating my chest and moaning," he said.

"Why don't you tell us all about it?"

"You wouldn't believe it. Nobody else did."

"Elias seems to," she said. "Your brother did."

Webb looked at her, startled. "My brother? How did you know about him?"

"I've heard the other side of the story," she said. "But not your side. That's what I'm trying to get out of you."

"You heard it from Sid Raines, of course?" Webb snapped.

"No. That's the last thing in the world I'd imagine he'd want to talk about. But it was all in the eastern newspapers three years ago."

"In the newspapers?"

"Of course," she said. "It all started with you being a hero. I read all about how Lieutenant Webb Jernegan fought a duel with the Pawnee chief, Brass Kettle. How he spared Brass Kettle's life, and how the Indians kept their word to spare the soldiers they had trapped in a buffalo wallow out on the plains."

Webb stared at her, dumfounded.

"Do you mean to say you didn't know your fame had spread that far?" she asked. "Why, you were even the hero in a melodrama on the stage in New York City. It was called *Lieutenant Jernegan's Fateful Day.*"

"Hold on!" Webb roared. "You're making this up."

"I'm not. I saw the play myself, even though ladies weren't supposed to be seen in such places. I was in New York with my father. He was there on business, outfitting for the trading trip to China. I dressed as a boy and went to the playhouse alone."

She added, "It was thrilling. The duel with Brass Kettle was—" She paused, eying him in mock alarm. "You look ill."

"I'm sick as a dog," Webb said. "This isn't true, is it?"

"I'm afraid it is," she said. "They were naming babies after you. That was what Loa was talking about a moment ago."

"Babies!" Webb clapped a hand to his forehead. "Babies! After me? Now that's the living end!"

He glared at her. "Did the papers print what happened afterward?"

"You mean your court-martial? Of course."

"Well, now, that must have been a shock to giddy girls, such as the kind that dress like boys and go to see shoddy melodramas."

"It was," she said demurely. "I was desolate—for hours. As a matter of fact it was an even greater sensation than the story of the duel."

"Naturally," Webb said. "The fallen hero. What happened to the play?"

"It closed immediately," she said. "The papers

in New York sent special correspondents to Fort Leavenworth to write about your court-martial. It was a nine-day wonder. The idol smashed. The feet of clay. Webb Jernegan, the conqueror of Brass Kettle, a thief! A murderer! Betrayer of his oath of office."

"You don't have to spread it on that thick," Webb snarled. "What did they do with the babies you said people named for me? Did they drown 'em?"

She threw back her head and laughed. It was the first time she had really thrown off strain and tension since he had encountered her in Yerba Buena.

Loa joined in. Elias began laughing, too. With Elias it built up into an earthquake. He rolled on the ground, kicking the earth with his heels, gasping for breath.

Madge recovered. "That was good for me," she said. "Good for us all."

"But hard on the babies," Webb said. "I suppose the newspapers were in a rage when the word got out that I had escaped."

She nodded. "That was another terrific sensation."

"It'll raise some more goose-pimples on them back east if we're caught," Webb said. "Eli will be in as deep as me. He's the one who slugged a couple of sentries and got me out of that cell at Leavenworth."

"The guards were easy to slug," Elias said. "They were soldiers who had served under Sid Raines. They knew Webb had been given a raw deal. They hadn't forgot that he'd saved the lives of men in the ranks by fightin' that duel with Brass Kettle."

"The Army knows Elias got me out," Webb said. "It's a death offense to help a condemned prisoner escape. In addition to that, my brother is still in prison. He was given twenty years."

"As bait," Elias said.

"Bait?" Madge asked.

"It's Webb the Army wants. They know he's tried twice to get Terry out. They know he'll try ag'in. They'll be layin' for him."

"But it's not necessary now," Madge exclaimed. "That's what I've been trying to make him understand. There's no more need for haunting. There are no more hobgoblins. Raines is alive and you can prove it. Loa and I can swear to it."

"You've got only our word that he *is* Raines," Webb said. "Maybe we're hoodwinking you. Maybe he isn't Raines at all and we're running a scheme to trick you into giving false testimony."

She looked at him helplessly. "Now, that's not possible. The—"

"I know the Army," Webb said. "They'll have to see Raines in the flesh before they'll believe he's alive. And we're a long way from Fort Leavenworth."

"We still haven't heard your side of it," she said. "As I remember it, you were accused of murdering your superior officer to cover up embezzlement and theft from the Army. You were a supply officer for the troops stationed at posts on the Santa Fe Trail, and you falsified records, engaged in illegal deals with traders and were tied up with a gang of Mexican bandits and crooked merchants at Santa Fe who acted as fences for Army goods you diverted to them."

"You seem to have been a close follower of sensational newspaper stories," Webb commented. "You have a good memory."

Loa giggled. "My sister, I think, had the big, what you call it, big smash on Lieutenant Jernegan because of his duel with the chief of the savages."

"Crush, not smash," Elias said. He eyed Madge tolerantly. "I guess gals *do* get soft about characters they read about in the papers."

"Proceed with the story," Madge said, her cheeks fiery. "And keep me out of it."

"It was Raines who juggled the books," Webb said. "He set up the whole framework for handling supplies between Fort Leavenworth and Mexican territory. He was commanding officer at Diamond Cantonment. I was officially named on the orders he had made out as supply officer, but I didn't know that until later. Raines really handled that job. He always was sharp at figures, and a born horse trader. But he forged or made out all official orders so that it appeared I was back of all the off-color deals. I was, in fact, on field duty the biggest part of the time, escorting wagon trains or scouting, when according to the records I was buying supplies. Stealing them, rather, or sending word to outlaws where they could be stolen."

"Yes," Madge said. "Sharp dealing comes naturally to Raines. I found that out at Yerba Buena when I made the mistake of buying supplies from him for the ship."

"And murder, too, is in his line when necessary," Webb said. "He'll kill. He found out that I had got suspicious of what was going on. He knew I'd pin it on him. He was in so deep he couldn't wriggle out if ever an official inquiry started. It happened that the Army paymaster was coming through from Leavenworth to pay off the troops at posts along the trail. Pay was three months overdue because of some snag back in Washington, so the pay wagon was carrying three times the usual amount. More than twenty-five thousand dollars. In gold eagles. The Army always pays in gold."

Webb rubbed the bristle of beard on his chin. "I wish I had a razor," he said. "They itch. Anyway, Raines knew the money was coming through. It was routine to send an officer up the trail from Diamond Cantonment to meet the pay wagon at Bridge Creek where it crossed into the district for which Raines was responsible. That officer reached Bridge Creek after dark. He introduced himself to the paymaster as Lieutenant Webb Jernegan."

"But this man was this Sidney Raines?" Loa exclaimed.

"I'm sure it was," Webb said. "He was wearing one of my uniforms. His own were tailor-made, but I couldn't afford that. We're about the same height and build. In those days, I sported a little wisp of mustache. Raines had a fine, long waxed mustache and sideburns. It was easy to shave off the sideburns and trim down the size of the mustache. A little lampblack or soot would have darkened his hair enough to get by under candle-light in a tent, which is about the only look anybody got of him. And I imagine he was careful to make sure they didn't get too much of a look in direct light."

Webb sat for a moment, staring off into the distance, remembering. "The paymaster was a Major George Anderson, newly assigned to the plains. He did not know either me or Raines. My counsel brought that out at the court-martial. Anderson had with him a detail of six Dragoons as escort. During the night their camp was hit by men dressed as Indians. The major was killed, along with three of the detail. Three Dragoons escaped, but they bumped into hostile Indians before they got back to Leavenworth, and only two of them made it alive. The pay wagon was found burned. The money was gone."

"The two soldiers who got back to Leavenworth identified you on the witness stand as the officer who came to the camp that night, as I recall it," Madge said.

"Yes. They believed they were telling the truth. But it was only their imagination. I was nearly a hundred miles away at the time. Raines had sent me out alone to locate a supposed war party of Comanches that he said were reported to have come up from the Staked Plains to prey on Santa Fe caravans. But when the orders of the day were read, Raines had made them out to show that I was the officer who had been detailed to meet the pay wagon at Bridge Creek."

"He had sent you into Indian country again, and this time alone?" Madge asked.

"This was different from the Brass Kettle thing," Webb said. "I saw nothing wrong with this detail. As a matter of fact, a man alone wasn't in much danger, if he was experienced in the Indian country and was careful. It was when we had half a dozen troopers kicking up dust that we got into the trouble with the Pawnees on that other occasion."

He shrugged wryly. "I didn't know until

afterward that I wasn't in danger from Indians at all. There were no Comanches. The buffalo-hunting season was over. But it just about cost me my neck anyway. Raines's object in sending me into vacant country alone was to make sure there'd be nobody to corroborate the fact that I was a long distance away when the pay wagon was robbed.

"I was making a siwash camp near the Arickaree River when a detail of civilian scouts and Delaware Indians, who'd been sent out to trail me down, came in on me as I was asleep and arrested me."

"What is it, this siwash camp?" Loa asked. "I do not comprehend."

"The sky and your belly for a blanket," Webb explained. "The buffalo grass for a mattress. But, as I was saying—"

"What is it, this bellee?" Loa inquired.

"Never mind," Webb said. "You *do* ask questions, don't you? As I was saying, I was taken back to the cantonment, charged with embezzlement, robbery and murder. They had found money in my saddlebags when they arrested me on the Arickaree. Only about eighty dollars. I didn't know it was there. It was in gold eagles. And while they couldn't legally identify it in the court-martial as part of the payroll, everybody in the room believed it. That, as much as anything, convicted me. The money had been planted by Raines, of course, when he sent me on that scouting trip. That was my only explanation, which nobody believed. It was pointed out that, not having been paid in three months, I should have been broke, like all the other officers, including Raines. And the same went for my brother."

"But—" Madge began.

Webb raised a hand, halting her. "You asked for the whole story. Here it is. Raines had disappeared at the time of the robbery. They found in his desk at the cantonment a sealed letter which carried instructions that it was to be opened only in case of his death by violence.

"In it Raines had written that he had evidence that Terry and I had been stealing from the Army and were in partnership with Mexican thieves. He said he believed we suspected that he was suspicious of us, and that we might try to silence him before he could gather complete evidence and arrest us."

Webb smiled grimly. "Oh, Sid did it up brown, all right. He wrapped me and Terry up neat and tight. The one thing he couldn't produce was his own dead body. But he did a pretty good job of making people imagine they'd seen even that. His horse was found, saddled but with no rider, wandering ten miles out from the post near a big marsh along the Neosho River. There was a bullet gouge on the saddle. One of Raines's boots was found, with bloodstains in it. They dragged the boghole. They found only Raines's hat. But a dozen bodies could have been sunk there and never found. Everybody knew that."

Webb lifted another chunk of skewered salt pork, tested it and recoiled from its scorching touch. "Cuss it," he exclaimed. "Blistered my tongue."

"Why did Raines involve your brother?" Madge asked.

It was Elias who answered that. "These bullheaded Jernegans sort o' cling together. An' hang together. Raines planted some more money in Terry's quarters at the cantonment. It was found when he was arrested on the strength o' Raines's letter. They figured Webb an' Terry had cached the main part of the pay money. They gave Terry twenty years. That must have disappointed Raines almost as much as when Webb got loose from prison. For Sid knew better'n to frame Webb an' not Terry. He knew that if either of 'em was loose, they'd never give up huntin' him, not even after twenty years."

"And one of them *is* loose and has found him after three years," Madge said.

"I would have swung, except for Eli and his friends," Webb said. "Eli and I made it across the Arkansas into Mexican territory. We toughed it out there. I tried twice to get Terry out, but bungled it both times. A trapper friend of Eli's finally gave us the information we wanted. He mentioned that he'd seen a man in a settlement named Yerba Buena in California who looked like an Army captain he'd known when he was scouting on the plains. Sidney Raines. That was two months ago, at Taos. And so here we are."

Chapter Nine

They all sat silent for a time, the girls sinking back, the weariness returning.

"And now Raines has slipped away from you again," Madge finally said.

"Maybe," Webb said. Presently he added, "Maybe not. I've got to get Terry out of prison. Sometimes when I get to thinking about him in a cell I get to sweating. I almost go crazy. I've failed him."

"I must find Raines too," Madge said.

Webb looked at her. "The bag of pretty stones?" he asked harshly.

"Yes."

"You mean you've got regrets?" he demanded.

"Regrets?"

"Do you mean you think they were worth more than what you got for them?"

She sat straight up, sudden outrage flaring in her eyes. "I see what you're driving at! You're asking me if I regret that you gave them up to save Loa from torture."

In Webb was dull anger—but greater than that was bitter disappointment. He had expected more of this amber-eyed, direct-talking person. "They wouldn't have stopped with Loa, you know," he said. "If they couldn't have gotten the information they wanted from her, you'd have been the next to have been toasted in front of that fire. You *do* know that, of course?"

"Certainly I know it. But you asked me if I had regrets. I do."

"What good would that bag of pretty stones do you in your grave?" Webb demanded.

"I'd have given them and a thousand bags like them, if I could have helped Loa last night," she said. "What kind of a person do you think I am?"

"You tell me."

She gazed at him with scorn. "You can go to the devil," she said. She returned to the task of braiding her hair, ignoring him.

"It happens that I am well acquainted with the devil," Webb said. "You're a little late. I've already gone to that source for help."

"I can believe that," she said.

Loa spoke. "The precious stones were not my sister's to give away, señor. She had already told you that."

Webb and Elias eyed her. She nodded. "They belong to the people of a place called Goodhaven. I was to this place when I was a young girl. I visited there with my sister when I went to America on a voyage with her father in his cleeper sheep."

"Clipper ship, dear," Madge said.

"Cleeper sheep. That is what I say. This place,

this Goodhaven, it is a little village in—in—I cannot say this word. It is so big."

"Massachusetts, Miss Loa," Elias said. "I've been in Goodhaven. It's a whalin' town. That's where that craft, in which we went on the beach, was named."

"What happened to the original *Goodhaven*?" Webb asked.

"It is gone," Loa sighed. "It is at the bottom of the sea. In the Straits of Sundra."

"My father, Nathaniel Peary, was captain of the clipper ship," Madge said. "But he wasn't the owner. He only had a share in it. The original *Goodhaven* was owned by all of the people of our village. One hundred and twenty-four citizens of Goodhaven mortgaged property, borrowed or scraped together enough money to build the *Goodhaven* and outfit her for the China trade. The crew were all Goodhaven men."

She paused for a time, then went on. "They're all gone now. The most of them are dead. The rest are deserters or worse. As far as the village is concerned, they're dead also. Twenty men, in addition to my father and Loa's parents. There are many women in Goodhaven who are widows but don't know it yet."

"How did it happen?" Webb asked quietly.

"What you really want to know," she said wearily, "is whether my father was a pirate, like Raines said that night in Yerba Buena."

151

"Was he a pirate?" Webb asked.

"I sailed with my father on his last voyage as captain of the *Goodhaven*," she said. "Mother had died when I was fourteen. It was an easy voyage in a good ship. We made it around the Horn to California and took on furs—mainly sea otter and fur seal—in trade for metal and hardware and tobacco that we had brought from the east coast. Furs are cheap and plentiful in California. Even sea otter. But in China and in Yeddo—that's in Japan—they bring high prices. The mandarins and Manchu princes especially value otter fur."

"So I've heard," Elias nodded. "Beaver don't pay for the stick to mark a trap, but they say there's still money in sea otter if you can get it to the heathen countries to—"

He realized his mistake, and looked at Loa in awful consternation.

She was puzzled. "But is it not this America that is heathen?" she asked.

Webb suddenly bent and kissed her on the cheek. "Of course," he said. "But we'll discuss it another time. I still haven't heard whether Nathaniel Peary was a pirate."

"You recall that I told you that my father and Loa's father were partners in the China trade. Juan Martinique operated small vessels that reached ports which deepwater ships never saw. My father gathered up what he brought from the interior and carried it back to America. It made an ideal arrangement. Our families were not only partners in business, but very close friends."

"Very, very good friends," Loa said, beaming.

"On this trip, Loa came with her parents to meet us at Singapore, which the British took over a few years ago. She stayed with me on the *Goodhaven* as we sailed the coast, loading. We took on spices and wonderful oriental lace and tea, ebony and silk. My father and Señor Martinique said it was the best year they'd ever known. Dad estimated that the *Goodhaven* would pay its investment back ten times over on that single voyage. The people of Goodhaven would no longer be in want, for the first time in their lives. They deserved it. Luck had always run against Goodhaven ships in the past. The village had lived a hard-scrabble existence."

She remained silent for a time and Webb could see that she was suddenly fighting back tears. "But the *Goodhaven* never got home with that rich cargo," she finally said. "We were boarded by Malay pirates in the Straits of Sundra. The biggest part of our crew were killed in the fight. Both Loa's father and her mother were killed. My father was wounded. The pirates set us survivors adrift in an open boat. They looted the *Goodhaven*, then set fire to it and scuttled it."

"We had a very, very bad time in that boat," Loa

said simply. "We had no water for days, no. It was very bad. *Muy malo.*"

"There were only eight of us, including Loa, myself and my father in the boat," Madge said. "We were all that was left of the clipper ship *Goodhaven.* We were adrift nearly a week before we made a landing on an island. We managed to survive there until father recovered."

"He was a fine man," Loa said reverently. "One of the *gente fino.* I pray for him, and for my *madre* and my *padre.* I weep for them."

"Father and the men captured a native fishing boat and forced the crew to sail them to the village the pirates had come from," Madge went on. "It was on an island off the Malay coast. Father and his men made their way through the jungle at night into the village and captured the pirate leaders. These men were living in luxury in ornate establishments, with many concubines. They owned fortunes in jewels and gold—all stolen in years gone by. Father took what you saw in the chamois bag. Pearls. A few rubies and other stones. Some tiny jade figures, stolen from Chinese temples."

She watched Webb, seeking some expression of criticism. "I'm not saying it was the most ethical thing imaginable," she said. "It was an eye for an eye. Nathaniel Peary never was a man to turn the other cheek. You should understand that."

"Now why do you say that?"

"Because you think and act exactly as my father did when it comes to dealing with people who've wronged you. What my father took from those thieves was barely enough to pay for the *Goodhaven* and its cargo. He could have taken more. Much more. He hardly touched the surface of the loot those pirates possessed."

"So he pirated the pirates," Webb said.

"That's only a play on words. Those gems didn't belong to those thieves. Who can say who owned them."

"I know who owns them now," Webb said. "Sid Raines. And Strapp."

"Father paid for them with his life," she said. "He set fire to the village. He and his men had to fight their way out. Only a few of them got back to the fishing boat. Father had been wounded again. He died after we reached the Straits Settlements. Only three of the men survived. They had filled their pockets with gems at the pirate village."

Webb looked at her, waiting. She nodded. "Wealth was too much for them. They refused to share with their neighbors back in Goodhaven. They disappeared at Singapore. Loa and I bought that old ship that you know about. It was the only vessel we could come upon. We named it the *Goodhaven* in memory of our parents. We could find only one person who was qualified to captain and navigate a vessel. Jed Strapp. He signed on his own crew and we sailed for America. You know the rest of it."

"Strapp, of course, knew you had the pouch of pretty stones aboard?" Webb asked.

Madge shrugged. "Of course. Father's raid on the pirate village was common knowledge before we sailed from Singapore."

Webb and Elias looked wryly at each other. "An' I was moanin' about us gittin' the rough side of it," Elias sighed.

Webb fished in a pocket and brought out two small items, which he handed to Madge. They were pearls.

"I held out on Raines," he said. "These two sort of stuck to my fingers while I was dribbling the stones back and forth when they were trying to toast Loa. It occurred to me that we might need them." He added, "But, it seems, they belong to the people of Goodhaven."

She looked at the gems in her palm. "You could have had them all," she said slowly.

"That was my first thought when I saw you hide them in that cubbyhole on the ship," Webb said.

"You're a good judge of value," she said. "These two are of fine quality."

Webb shrugged. "That was luck. How much are they worth?"

"That's hard to say. Possibly a thousand dollars each in the right market."

"That'll be enough to buy passage for you and Miss Loa back to Goodhaven," he said. "We'll make arrangements to see that you get to Yerba Buena. You should be able to find a ship leaving from there sooner or later."

She put the finishing touches to the thick braid of hair she had formed. "And you?" she asked.

"We might head in that direction too. Or we might not. It depends."

"On which way Sidney Raines's trail takes you?"

Webb nodded. He kicked earth over the fire and repacked their remaining food. "We're bound to find some sign of civilization soon," he said. "We'll keep going inland. There must be Spanish ranchos around here. There's a road I heard about that the padres built from mission to mission called El Camino Real. We ought to strike it if we keep heading east. There'll be travel on it. Maybe even stagecoach travel."

He eyed their footwear dubiously. The shoes the girls wore had been serviceable enough, but, like his boots and Elias's moccasins, had fared none too well from immersion in sea water.

"Looks like we'll be really afoot before long," he commented.

He drew Elias aside. "I'll circle around and see if I can pick up sign of which way the other outfit headed. I figure they'll have to go inland too, but we've got to make sure. That big draw ahead looks like it might lead through the hills. I'll catch up with the rest of you there."

He left them and headed through the brush. In less than a mile, he found what he sought. The trail Raines and his companions had left was twelve hours old or more, but easy to trace out. It was evident they had lost no time the previous night in pulling out from the beach, preferring speed and placing distance between themselves and Webb and Elias, rather than slowing their progress by trying to blind their trail.

They had followed the natural run of the land and this had led them to the break in the hills that Webb had pointed out as probably offering the easiest path among the maze of ridges.

Webb rejoined Elias and the girls. Even to the untrained eyes of Madge and Loa there was no mistaking the occasional footprints they came upon in sandy stretches along the stream they were following.

They had started out at the slogging pace of travelers who know they have a long way to go, but Madge, who had moved past Elias into the lead, without realizing it, was stepping up the gait.

"Whoa-up there, lady-gal," Elias remonstrated. "You act like you was just rememberin' somethin' you'd mislaid somewhere ahead."

"Yes," she said. "A bag of pretty stones."

"Gettin' all fagged out right at the start of a

hunt won't do to fetch meat for the pot," Elias said. "Nor pretty stones."

"It's better than snailing along," she said, her voice rising. "They're miles ahead already and probably gaining every minute. If you don't intend to catch them, then I do."

Webb overtook her and laid a hand on her arm. "Easy!" he said. "This might be a long trail. A mighty long one. And just what would we do if we ran them down right now? They're pretty well armed. There are four of them."

She wrested away from him. But she had no answer and realized it. Tears of frustration and despair began running down her face.

"Those poor people back home," she sobbed. "Friends. Neighbors. If I could have got back to Goodhaven with the ship and those stones it would have meant so much to them. So very much. They'd have been out of debt and would have made a fair profit. Now, all they'll have is more debt and disappointment. First I lost the ship. And then the stones."

There was nothing Webb could think of that seemed to be worthwhile. They moved ahead and she dried her tears.

Presently he realized that he had moved into the lead and had lengthened his stride, contrary to his better judgment. He looked guiltily at Elias, who shrugged but offered no objection. So he continued to set the faster gait, even though he believed that this chase would turn out to be a matter of endurance rather than speed. And luck. Above all, luck.

"Have you any idea where we are?" he asked Madge.

"I can only guess. I'd say we were driven ashore at least two hundred miles south of San Francisco Bay. We probably are in that stretch where the California coast begins to swing southeast. It makes quite a turn."

"What would be the nearest place where Raines might have a chance of boarding a deepwater ship?"

Madge thought that over, pursing her lips as she tried to visualize a map in her mind. "That probably would be a place called Buenaventura," she said. "If I'm guessing right about where we now are, Buenaventura would be nearly a hundred miles south of here. My father put the original *Goodhaven* in there to trade for fresh meat and vegetables when we were on our way to China. It's a fishing village built around a mission church. There are big ranchos in the back country that ship hides and tallow."

"Nothing closer than that?"

"I recall them saying there was a place called Santa Barbara not far up the coast, but it seemed to be a dangerous anchorage for ships. Few ever stopped there."

"How about in the other direction? North?"

"I don't recall any place where deepwater ships could find anchorage this side of Monterey Bay," she said. "That's well up the coast toward San Francisco Bay."

"Monterey is the California capital," Webb said. "I doubt if *americanos* would be welcome there, from what we learned at Sutter's Fort."

The surroundings became more rugged, but they followed the sandy bed of the creek, which had cut an arroyo through the hills. The stream had dwindled to a trickle as they moved deeper into the hills. It vanished often in the sands, reappearing here and there in the form of small pools and reedy marshes.

They had left the fogs and winds of the sea behind them. This was a warmer, brighter country. The sun rose and began to beat down on them as the morning advanced.

Noon came. Midafternoon. They gnawed occasionally at hardtack and paused at times to drink where the stream ran fresh. The arroyo wound endlessly along the bases of beetling hills where thickets of wild roses and wild lilac bloomed among the chaparral.

Sycamores began to appear along the creek. Clearings broke the monotony of the chaparral where live oaks, wearing gray beards of Spanish moss, grew in open parks. They began to sight cattle trails in the brush, but the cattle themselves kept out of sight.

They traveled in silence. The girls uttered no complaint, but they were forcing themselves to keep pace. Webb had long since slowed and shortened his stride in order to spare them.

He spoke the first words in nearly an hour, voicing a thought he had been turning over in his mind. "Raines will know we'll figure him as heading for a seaport. What if he takes another direction—overland?"

" 'Tain't likely he'd try anything like that," Elias said. "Not by way o' Carson's trace an' the Great Basin. That's American territory an' he might bump into somebody who'd recognize him. He knows he'll be hung if he shows up in any place the Army can get him."

"How about him staying in Mexican territory?"

"If you mean he'd head overland by way of the Gila River trail, them Yuma an' Papago tribes would have his scalp in no time, from what I've been told. That's no route for only four men to travel. Raines must know that."

"How about the Spanish Trail?"

"The *jornada*?"

There was something in Elias's voice that caused the girls to look questioningly at him.

"Why not?" Webb demanded. "Raines is no greenhorn. He's traveled *jornadas*. Some tough ones."

"His partners never have, you can bet on that," Elias snorted. "They're seamen."

"Where is this *jornada*?" Loa asked.

"The stretch across a desert called the Mojave to the Rio Colorado and a hundred or so miles beyond," Webb said. "I've never been on it, but trappers have told me about it."

"An' none of 'em ever wanted to have any part of that *jornada* ag'in," Elias said.

"There are plenty of *jornadas* in the southwest," Webb explained for the benefit of Madge and Loa. "There's one the traders travel south of Santa Fe on the road to Chihuahua that the Spanish call the Jornada del Muerto. Journey of death. I've been over that one, scouting and meat-hunting for trading caravans. It's lined with the bones of cattle and horses. Graves too. No water for ninety miles. Another rough one is the cutoff south of the Arkansas River that Santa Fe traders sometimes use in years of good rains. But some men, who've been over all of them, say this *jornada* across California can be the worst of all. Especially now, with full summer coming on."

"Raines wouldn't travel the *jornada*, even if the Old One was at his heels," Elias declared.

That brought silence. Webb looked at them and said, "All right. It's been said before. The devil *is* after him."

"Don't talk like that," Madge protested.

"What should I talk like?" Webb asked.

"It's—it's sacrilegious."

"I'll pray for you," Loa said. "You are a lost soul."

"Before we're through with this," he said, "the rest of you may lose your souls too. I'm following him, wherever he goes."

They slogged ahead, and now it was an effort to lift a foot for each step.

Webb halted, peering. The arroyo had widened into a sunbaked, dry expanse of sand. The footprints Raines and his companions had made were blotted out by the tracks of the hoofs of horses. They were unshod hoofs, but these horses had been carrying riders, for there were the marks of boot heels in the sand. Webb saw the spider trails that had been made by big Spanish spurs.

"*Vaqueros*," he said. "They came out of the chaparral and intercepted Raines's bunch. From the looks, they took all four with them, riding double."

They moved ahead. They left the sand flat and made their way for a mile or more through an open stand of gnarled oaks. Abruptly, they emerged into view of a mighty valley, green and lush under the clear sunlight. It stretched north and south as far as the eye could carry. To the east rose another range of broken hills.

A road formed a yellow thread the length of the valley. "El Camino Real," Webb said.

To the south they could make out what evidently was one of the mission churches the padres had built. It was surrounded by fields that had been cleared and cultivated, but these seemed deserted now and there was no sign of life around the church.

Nearer at hand, very distinct in the clear air but at least five miles away, stood the headquarters of a rich California rancho. Its *casa*, or main house, was low and rambling, with tile roofs and galleries and whitewashed adobe walls, vine-clad and shaded by trees. A cluster of other structures and corrals were scattered over a considerable area.

A *fiesta* seemed to be in progress, for the rancho's compound swarmed with people and activity. Bunting and banners fluttered. Horses crowded the corrals and pastures.

Some sort of an equestrian contest was going on and was the center of attention.

As they stood staring, riders who had been waiting, hidden among the oaks, swooped into view and surrounded them. They were vaqueros, brown-faced, black-haired, mustachioed men, garbed for the *fiesta* in colorful blouses, brocaded jackets and leather breeches. Hawk bells and silver ornaments jingled on their hatbrims. They were whirling *reatas*.

Webb snatched for his pistol, but too late.

Chapter Ten

Webb felt a loop settle over his shoulders, flipped by a vaquero who had circled back of him. It tightened. He had his pistol drawn and probably could have killed the man with the rope. He held his fire.

He was dragged off his feet, but the vaquero, a little frightened, realized that he had been spared from death, halted his horse and slackened the *reata*, which was snubbed around a low saddle horn of a size that would have taken both hands to span. Webb had heard that California vaqueros used lariats of amazing length and snubbed down cattle by hand, taking a turn of the rope around the saddle horn and playing the animal by hand.

Webb shrugged off the loop and leaped to his feet. Elias had been roped also. He had not drawn his pistol. He braced his legs. As the vaquero wrapped a dally around the horn and prepared to topple him, he acted first, leaning back, tightening the rope with a mighty heave. Instead of going down himself, he toppled horse and vaquero, bringing them down in a tangle of hoofs and arms and legs.

Elias wriggled out of the loop. The horse, unhurt, scrambled to its feet. Elias caught the vaquero by the belt and the seat of his pants, lifted him as he would a child high in the air, then plopped him back in the saddle with a teeth-jarring thud.

"There you are, little one," he said, using his deepest voice. "Next time, try to stay on your horse. An' if I ever catch you whirlin' that piece o' string in my direction ag'in, I'll take it away from you an' give you a good hidin'."

A roar of laughter burst from the other vaqueros. If they didn't understand Elias's words, his meaning was plain. They pointed at their humiliated *compañero*, casting jibes until finally he also began to grin sheepishly.

They quit laughing abruptly when one of their number uttered a sharp order, as though evidently realizing that this was not the thing to do under the circumstances.

However there was respect in all of them, and even in the voice of the one who seemed to be in authority. He was an older vaquero than the others, seamed and leathery.

He addressed them in harsh, peremptory words. But his rapid Spanish was too much for Webb or Elias.

It was Loa who answered for them. She snapped her fingers scornfully under the nose of the spokesman, halting him in midsentence. "No!" she said loftily.

Her eyes flashing, she followed that refusal

with a blast of Spanish that caused her victim to retreat a step. The other vaqueros blinked. They straightened in the saddles and removed their sombreros. They were suddenly respectfully attentive.

"What is it?" Webb asked. "What did he say to us?"

"This man, this *pelado*, say we are under arrest for invading Mexican territory," Loa said. "He says it is by order of his *patron*, Don Pasquel Molino. It is Don Pasquel's rancho that we see."

Webb placed his pistol back in his belt. "All right," he said. "That's where we want to go anyway. As for being under arrest, that shouldn't be hard to straighten out."

Loa explained to the vaqueros. They beamed, evidently much relieved when they understood that the *americanos* were not in the mood to make trouble.

They were given horses. Vaqueros helped Madge and Loa into saddles and leaped up to ride double with companions.

Elias was given the biggest animal in the party and even that mount was barely adequate for the task. The vaqueros continued to gaze at him with awe.

The rider he had manhandled began to look upon himself as a brave one who had bearded the dragon in its den and had escaped alive. He kept talking volubly to the others, evidently describing, with gestures, his thoughts and reactions during those terrible moments when he and his horse had been plucked off their feet by this giant, this human ogre.

"Why do they want to arrest us?" Madge asked Loa.

"I do not know. It is something about war between their country and your *Estados Unidos.*"

Webb frowned. "War? Do you suppose it's really gone that far?"

"I've heard stories about prisons in this part o' the world," Elias said darkly. "I don't hanker to find out for myself how bad they are."

The horses rushed along at a gallop. The girls, forced to ride sidewise in the stock saddles, clung desperately to horns and manes. "Horseback riding doesn't seem to be among our accomplishments," Madge stuttered dismally between jolts. "I never got nearer one of these things than the old dappled mare that used to be our buggy horse when I was a child in Goodhaven."

"I have ride the elephants in Java with my father and my mother," Loa chattered. "It was the best way in the jungle. It would often make me sick at my stomach. Very sick. But this is worse. Much worse. This *caballo* will beat me into little pieces."

The leader of the vaqueros understood two words of what Loa had said. *"Elefante?"* he inquired, gazing at Loa with new wonder and awe. "Javanese?"

She said haughtily, "*Si!*" She looked down her nose at him, abashing him into silence. She said imperiously, "*Mas despacio.* More slowly, please. *Muy polvo.* The dust is too much."

The vaqueros slowed the horses to a gait that was more endurable for herself and Madge.

"*Gracias*, princess," Madge said. And suddenly, despite their plight, they both giggled.

Webb peered as they approached the rancho. Guitars and mandolins were thrumming, and a drum was sounding softly. The guests were dancing on a hard-packed surface beneath huge, spreading valley oaks in the ranch yard, which faced the *galeria* of the main house. Water sparkled in irrigation ditches and splashed in a fountain. Fish swam lazily in a pond.

The dancing halted abruptly when their arrival was discovered. They were the center of curious but silent attention as the vaqueros guided the horses among the bystanders to the saddle step at the *galeria.*

Webb and Elias dismounted and helped the girls down. The *caporal* of the vaqueros beckoned them with a finger and led them into the house, down a wide, tiled hallway and into a room with beamed ceiling and whitewashed walls.

They blinked, for the room was dim and cool after the glare of the setting sun. They found themselves facing a dignified, aristocratic man in *charro* garb, who sat alone at a heavy, oak table. The room evidently served as a business office for the rancho.

They were being estimated by frosty gray eyes beneath thin, gray brows. The man was perhaps seventy, Webb judged, but lean and lithe and brown, and palpably had spent a great part of his life in a saddle.

His steeple-crowned sombrero lay on the table. It was bangled with gold coins. He wore the velvet jacket, slashed, gold-trimmed trousers and white silk stockings of a *hacendado*. His shirt was of finest linen, with a collar of Barcelona lace. A silver-handled pistol and a dagger with mother-of-pearl forming the handle were thrust in his crimson sash.

He searchingly inspected the girls. There was scorn in him at first, but this changed. He seemed surprised and at a loss. It was obvious that his curiosity was aroused. But when his glance returned to Webb and Elias, it held only hostility and accusation.

Webb spoke to Loa. "Tell him, when he's finished with looking us over, that we'd stack up a lot better after a bath, a shave and some food. Tell him we are not thieves or beggars."

The stern-faced man halted Loa with a gesture. "I understand the *yanqui* language and speak it, although I am not proud of that accomplishment," he said. "I am Don Pasquel Molino. I know who you are. You are worse than thieves. You are spies for your Captain Frémont."

"Frémont?" Webb exclaimed. "That's ridiculous."

"Do not bother to lie. You were sent by him to prepare the way for his scheme to make California a part of your country. Our governor, General Castro, ordered him out of California months ago. But he is back. With his soldiers. You are his spies."

"Do we look like spies?"

"Do you deny that Captain Frémont sent you?" Don Pasquel demanded.

"Of course I deny it. I've met Frémont, but that was some years back, on the Missouri River, when—"

"I'm sure you've met him, señor. He is your superior officer, Lieutenant Jernegan."

"I was Lieutenant Jernegan," Webb said. "There's only one person who could have told you that. Sidney Raines."

"I know of no person of that name," Don Pasquel snapped. "My information came from my good friend, Señor Stevens."

"He is your good friend?"

There was irony in Webb's voice that caused Don Pasquel to stiffen. "I've had the pleasure of meeting him in business matters in his establishment at Yerba Buena," he said. "I have been a guest in his *casa* there. Yes, Señor Stevens is my friend."

"He's here?" Webb asked eagerly. "In this house?"

Don Pasquel studied him frowningly. "It is true, then," he said. "You do hate him. You intend to kill him."

"Where is he?" Webb demanded.

Don Pasquel waved that aside. "My vaqueros found him and three shipwrecked *compañeros* trying to find their way here in search of food and shelter. Señor Stevens told me that you and this huge man here, and these two señoritas probably would appear also. I gave orders that you be arrested and brought here to me."

"What else did this Señor Stevens tell you?" Webb asked.

"That you were commissioned by Captain Fremont to do away with him."

"Do away with him?"

"He has opposed your countrymen at Yerba Buena in their plotting to seize California. He was the friend of the Mexican authorities at the risk of his own life. He was a thorn in the side of you *americanos*. They had to get rid of him. So they sent you, because they knew you held a grudge from the past against him. You failed to murder him, but you set fire to his establishment. To escape assassination, he fled to a vessel that was sailing. You even followed him aboard that ship. And now, you've even followed him here to my *casa* to kill him. What a fiend you must be!"

Elias spoke angrily. "Danged if you don't have to admire Sid for the way he kin pull the long bow. He always could talk himself out of a tight fix in a hurry."

"You deny these things?" Don Pasquel demanded.

"Certainly we deny them," Webb said. "But will it do any good?"

"No!" Don Pasquel snapped. But, beneath his stern attitude, Webb sensed an uneasiness. Don Pasquel was not as sure of his ground as he pretended. It was also evident that he was not accustomed to being addressed as an equal by ragged, unshaven men who came as prisoners.

"As an officer in your army, you could be placed before a firing squad as a spy for entering Mexican territory in disguise," Don Pasquel said. "Or hung. Surely, you know that."

"I'm not in disguise," Webb said. "These rags, which have seen some rough doings, are the only clothes to my name. I've been a civilian for three years. Your Señor Stevens has a poor memory. Or rather, he's a very smooth liar. And how did he explain why these two young ladies are with us, if we are spies?"

"The fact they preferred to join you speaks for itself," Don Pasquel said. "I would not refer to them as ladies."

Loa spoke disdainfully. "So? We are not ladies?

174

And you—you strutting peacock. Posing as a grandee. I laugh. You are a cow herder. I have *castellano* blood in my veins. You are a drover of cattle. In you runs the blood of a peon."

Don Pasquel rose to his feet, towering over her, trying to intimidate her with his glare. "You are the first *castellano* I have ever noticed with oriental eyes," he said.

Madge spoke. "My sister's eyes are the eyes of her mother who was a lady in waiting to a queen. They are the eyes of royal birth. A princess."

"And you, señor, have the eyes of a *vaca de leche*," Loa said. "A milk cow."

Webb saw that Don Pasquel was suddenly trying to hide a smile. He was impressed by Loa's spirit and haughtiness.

"If you are Spanish, señorita, even any part of you, why are you with these enemies of our people?" he asked.

"They are not enemies," Loa said. "Where is this man you call Señor Stevens? He is lying. His brain is cunning. He is a *ladron*, a thief. And a coward. He tried to torture me. Let us face him. Take us to him. You will see who is telling the truth."

Don Pasquel stood at a loss, studying them. He seemed to grow still more unsure of himself. The *fiesta* had been resumed in the ranch yard. They could hear shouts, pounding hoofs, music and the laughter of women and children.

Don Pasquel suddenly walked to a small window in the rear of the room and motioned Webb and Elias to join him. He pointed. The window, set in the thick adobe walls, faced southward. A faint drift of dust was visible in the open flats off to the southeast, well away from El Camino Real whose yellow thread passed not far from the rancho. In the reflection of the sun, which had gone below the coastal mountains, the dust, like the clouds overhead, was golden in hue.

"That," said Don Pasquel, "is Señor Stevens and his party."

"What?" Webb exclaimed. "But you said—"

"I did not say he was still here. You only took that for granted. He and his *compañeros* rested here for a few hours. He still fears for his life, not only at your hands, but at the hands of others of your people. He has made many enemies among the *americanos* by opposing them."

"Waugh!" Elias snorted. "If you ask me, he was a friend o' you *californios* when he was with *californios*. When he was with *americanos*, he was backing them."

Don Pasquel shrugged. "In any event, he told me it was best to leave California at once."

"You gave him horses," Webb snapped. "And a pack animal or two, by the looks."

"Horses are plentiful," Don Pasquel said. "No guest leaves Casa Molino on foot."

"You're helping a scoundrel!" Madge exclaimed.

"How about furnishing Eli and myself with horses too?" Webb demanded. "We'll bring him back. Then you can judge for yourself who was lying."

"You are not guests," Don Pasquel said. "You are prisoners. However, I do not wish to have the *fiesta* marred by any unpleasantness. My friends are celebrating my birthday. It is a very great honor."

Madge walked to the table where Don Pasquel had been sitting and lifted the ornate sombrero that lay there. Beneath it, reposing on a silk handkerchief, was a beautiful pearl.

"It seems that your guests paid for their horses and paid well," she said.

Don Pasquel snatched up the pearl and pocketed it. "You presume!" he raged. "This was a present that Señor Stevens left with me to be given to my wife, the Doña Molina."

"And a very nice present it was," Webb said.

"Unfortunately, it wasn't his to give," Madge said. "It belongs to the people of my town. The village of Goodhaven, in the state of Massachusetts."

"What is this nonsense?" Don Pasquel snapped. "Señor Stevens told me he was given the pearl as payment for supplies sold to a Yankee ship owner at Yerba Buena."

"That part of it is true, at least," Madge said. "I

am the ship owner. Now if you will furnish us with horses, I also have a—"

Webb motioned her into silence. He realized she was intending to use the two pearls he had held out of the pouch as payment for riding stock. But this was not the time.

"We're ragged and hungry, señor," he said. "This can be talked over later. We need food and a bath. The ladies need rest."

Don Pasquel's manner changed. "Of course," he said. "I regret my rudeness." He bowed to the girls. "I do not make war on women. And, at *fiesta* time, all who come to my *casa* will share with us our good fortune. It is the California custom. You will be made comfortable for the night at least."

He clapped his hands, calling for *mozos*, who came hurrying. He gave rapid orders. Webb and Elias found themselves being prodded down an inner corridor at gunpoint by two vaqueros, with a servant leading the way.

They reached the open door of a room and were motioned to enter. Don Pasquel had followed them. "The señoritas will be made comfortable," he said. "Do not try to leave this room. You will be shot down. I have so ordered."

"You're letting a criminal get away," Webb said.

"I will think over your story later on," Don Pasquel said. "I must admit that I am puzzled. I want to be fair."

"Later on? Why not now? By morning he'll be that much farther out of reach."

"You mean you wish to pursue him now—tired and hungry as you are?"

"I've hunted him for three years," Webb exclaimed. "Do you think I'm happy about losing him now."

"Three years? You have pursued this man for that length of time?"

"If he slips through my fingers this time I might never cut his trail again. He'll hide deeper than he did before."

"It must be a bitter grudge, indeed, that you hold against him."

"How would you look at a man who had schemed to have you court-martialed and sentenced to be hung for his murder, and who had sent your brother to prison on false evidence? Eli, here, is likely to be hung too, if he's caught, for standing by me."

"Perhaps I should pray for both your soul and that of this man you accuse," Don Pasquel said ironically.

"Prayers won't bring him back. He's got to be dragged by the heels. He will be aboard a ship before we can catch him, if you try to hold us here. Maybe by tomorrow. The sea leaves no trail by which we could follow him."

"That is one path, at least, that's closed to him," Don Pasquel said. "All *yanqui* ships at San

179

Diego and Buenaventura have been seized by our government. Those at Monterey by this time also, no doubt."

"Seized?"

"War has broken out between our two countries. There has been fighting in Texas. A courier from San Diego passed by only last night. All *americanos* who cannot show a legal right to be in Mexican territory are to be arrested. In view of this, I advised Señor Stevens that—"

"Raines," Webb said. "His real name is Sidney Raines, former captain in the United States Dragoons."

"So be it," Don Pasquel said resignedly. "You are either speaking the truth or you are a good actor. In any event, he was my friend. At least he too seems to have told the truth when he said his life was in danger at your hands. I warned him of what was happening and that he would be thrown in prison if he appeared at Buenaventura or San Diego. He is not known to the California authorities in these places."

Don Pasquel paused and made a wry gesture. "I would not wish that upon even an enemy, let alone a friend. I am afraid our prisons are not pleasant places in which to spend time. That is why I outfitted him and his party with horses and food for an overland journey."

"Overland?" Webb exclaimed. "Which way . . . ?"

"I advised the Spanish Trail and sent a guide who knows that route."

"The Spanish Trail!" Webb breathed. "Now we've got a chance again of getting him. He'll probably try to make it to a Texas port or maybe New Orleans and find a ship where he can get out of the country."

"The Spanish Trail!" Elias groaned. "The *jornada*! Hell's highway!"

"Not so fast," Don Pasquel said. "You are more likely to find yourselves in a Mexico City dungeon. After the *fiesta*, I will hear your story and decide what to do."

"After the *fiesta*? When will that be?"

Don Pasquel shrugged. "Who knows? A few days. A week, perhaps. Two weeks. Until my guests leave. Many of them have not even arrived as yet. Some have come from a long distance to pay their respects. I will let nothing interfere with their pleasure."

He made a gesture, and the vaqueros entered and disarmed them. Don Pasquel moved to the door. "*Buenas noches*," he said. "Please make no trouble. There will be guards under the windows and in the *casa*."

The silver bells on his spur chains made tinkling music as he walked away. The door was closed and bolted.

Other music swelled up. The dancing was resumed in the ranch yard. Webb and Elias moved

181

to an opposite window. Their room was at the end of the west wing of the house. This window overlooked the *galeria* and the ranch yard.

Torches had been lighted. The shadows of the mountains had changed from lilac to deep purple, and this tide was moving through the entire valley. The coming darkness was balmy, sweet with the perfume of night-blooming plants.

Webb smashed a palm futilely against a wall. The wall was as unyielding as the velvet trap that had caught them, holding them while Raines built up distance.

"Days," he said hoarsely. "Weeks."

Chapter Eleven

Tubs of water were brought, along with razors and towels. Also clean dry clothes to replace their ragged garb. These were the coarse cotton blouses and baggy breeches of peons, but after they were bathed and dressed they felt like kings.

Food was served. It was the same savory food whose aroma drifted from the ranch yard where whole beeves were being roasted over charcoal pits. Flasks of *aguardiente* were brought. The servants who carried the trays were hostile at first toward these *yanquis*. But they began to soften and stare in awe as Elias continued to empty his plate.

"We had one piece of luck, at least," Elias stated as he tilted another cup of wine. "If we had to be caught, it was right nice that it happened at a time when the *patron* was feedin' everybody well—even *americanos*."

The *mozos* sighed happily when he finally reluctantly pushed back his bench. They left, swollen with the importance of the stories they could add to the list of tales about this *americano bárbaro*.

"If we're turned loose, it'll be because the *hacendado* can't afford to feed you any longer," Webb said.

"A fine way to put it over," Elias declared.

A chicken-pulling contest started in the ranch yard. They watched from the window. By torchlight, *caballeros* were taking turns riding at breakneck speed and leaning from the saddles to snatch the heads of fowls buried to the necks in sand. It was a bloody, savage sport that aroused wild, screaming uproar from onlookers, both male and female.

Webb eyed the horses the competitors rode. "If we could only get out of here and grab a couple of those *caballos*," he said longingly.

It was futile to even wish. There was no answer to the problem of how to contend with the armed men who guarded the windows and the door. In addition, Webb doubted that Elias could squeeze through either of the small windows, even if chance for escape by that route should present itself.

The chicken-pulling ended. After a lull, a new and greater excitement drew them back to the window. Savage snarling of a wild animal arose, along with the bellowing of a bull.

The center of interest was a sizable corral-like enclosure made of stout timbers, which had only a small, double trap gate as an entrance. The timbers towered some twelve feet, and were set inches apart so that the guests could see into the arena. A catwalk was built atop the circle of posts.

All other activity had halted. The *fiesta* guests

were crowding eagerly around the arena, peering between the timbers.

The snarling and bellowing swelled to a frenzied pitch. Webb and Elias got glimpses in the torch-light of what was going on in the enclosure.

"They've put a grizzly an' a black bull in there, fightin'," Elias muttered. "Looks like they've roped the critters together. I ain't got much stomach for watchin' that sort o' thing."

The battle went on to the accompaniment of the screams and yells of the onlookers and the blood-curdling sounds of beasts fighting to the death.

Abruptly the uproar ceased. There was a moment of silence, followed by laughter and shouting from the crowd.

After a time, with men forcing the bear back by using iron prod poles, the trap gate was swung open, and the carcass of the bull was dragged from the arena by an ox team. The bull's back had been broken, although it appeared to have been a big, powerful animal.

After the gate was closed they could see the grizzly still stalking around the enclosure, snarling and striking at the posts. The crowd shrank back, women screeching in mock alarm.

Some of the celebrants, the *aguardiente* racing in their blood, began poking prod poles between the timbers, or climbed to the catwalk swinging long bullwhips, goading the grizzly into greater fury.

Attention swung to a new point. Don Pasquel came walking across the *fiesta* grounds, leading a handsome *bayo*, or buckskin horse. It was a solid-barreled, short-coupled mount in top condition, equipped with only a halter and lead rope.

Don Pasquel tethered the buckskin to a post near the bear arena and made a short, smiling speech, with gestures.

The laughter died away into uneasy tittering. There was an awkward pause. Don Pasquel waited, then spoke jeeringly. He clapped his hands and beckoned. A vaquero came hurrying, carrying a new saddle, which he placed on the horse.

"It's a duel of some kind," Webb said. "He's trying to prod someone into taking him up on whatever it is. He's put up a horse and saddle as a prize."

Finally a man stepped out of the crowd and swaggered to the buckskin, slapping it on the flank, then thumping himself on the chest. He was a big, brawny-shouldered vaquero.

A second man joined him. This one was a vaquero also by his garb, but was small and sinewy. He carried a coiled *reata* in his hands.

The big man stripped off his *charro* jacket and shirt and stood bare to the waist. The spectators suddenly came to life.

"*Olé*! *Olé*! Pablo Escobar! *Viva*! *Viva*!"

Servants brought to Don Pasquel a wicked, glittering knife with a foot-long blade and a heavy bullhide shield similar to those Webb had seen Comanches carry into battle, but far bigger. These two implements were handed to Pablo Escobar.

The two vaqueros knelt and crossed themselves. Silence came as they walked to the arena, mounted the timbers to the catwalk and peered down at the snarling bear inside.

"Man ag'in grizzly," Elias said uneasily. "I've heard that these *californios* fight bears with nothin' but shields an' a knife. They call it sport. They've got plenty o' sand. I don't hanker to watch this. That grizzly's no runt, an' it's on the prod."

The smaller man with the *reata* was playing out his loop, waiting for the chance to make his cast. Deftly he flipped the rope. A burst of snarling fury told that he had caught the grizzly.

Instantly, the big man dropped into the arena, armed only with the shield and knife. The fury of the bear increased. Dust arose, and the onlookers froze into terrified silence.

The man on the parapet strained at the *reata*, seeking to help his comrade by giving the bear two opponents to think about. Webb suddenly felt cold sweat break out on him. It was evident that something had gone wrong.

The man on the parapet began screeching in terror and redoubled his efforts. Men around the enclosure burst into frantic activity, using prod poles, evidently to divert the bear from some prey.

The gate was opened. Men rushed in and emerged carrying the big vaquero. Pablo Escobar was bloody and unconscious. An arm hung crookedly limp. He was placed on a blanket and carried into the hacienda. He had lasted only a few seconds in the arena and had been badly mauled.

Infuriated, the spectators began torturing the grizzly. Whips and prod poles went into action again. Firebrands were hurled into the arena. Men began heating long iron poles with the intention of inflicting revenge on the bear for what had happened to Pablo Escobar.

Don Pasquel finally returned from the house, lifted a hand for silence and spoke in Spanish. Webb knew enough of the language to get the gist of what he was saying. Pablo Escobar would live, but it would be some time before he would be of a mind to fight a bear again.

Don Pasquel paused for a moment. He turned and gazed toward Webb and Elias at the window from which they were peering. He gave an order and a vaquero soon appeared, leading a second buckskin horse that bore a saddle. It was a powerful animal, much bigger than the first *bayo*. Don Pasquel personally tethered it alongside the other horse and glanced toward the window again. There was a taunt in his manner as he turned his back and addressed the guests.

"The old snakeskin," Elias growled. "He's tryin'

to prod some other poor devil into gettin' chawed up by that bear."

"Yes," Webb said. "You or me."

"Now wait a minute! You're not sayin' . . . ?"

"That's what he's been after from the start. That's why he started putting up horses as prizes. He knows there's nothing we want more than horses. That big *bayo* he just brought out would make a good horse for you. He'd like nothing better than to entertain his guests by having an *americano* or two torn up by the grizzly."

Webb raised his voice so that all could hear him. "How about raising the ante a little more, Don Pasquel?"

Attention swung to him. Don Pasquel came walking nearer.

"What is that you say?" There was a faint twist of satisfaction on Don Pasquel's stern lips. Webb knew he had guessed right. Don Pasquel had hoped to goad him into taking up the challenge.

"Is a man's life worth only two horses and saddles?" Webb asked scornfully.

"Exactly what value do you put on your life?" Don Pasquel asked.

"One more *caballo* to carry our packs," Webb said. "The return of the arms and powder you took from us. We could use another rifle. Also food and something in which to cook it. And blankets."

"You ask very much."

"I value my blood highly, señor," Webb said.

"Are you saying you will fight the bear?"

"If it is made worthwhile."

"And these things you name? They are worthwhile?"

"Also to be allowed to pull out of here tonight," Webb said.

"I fear you will be in no condition to do so if you are foolish enough to try to fight the bear."

"That," Webb said, "is why it ought to be worth what I ask, to see me try. You have no love for *americanos*. It will give you and your guests considerable amusement to see our blood spilled."

"That is true," Don Pasquel said icily. "You mean you will fight the bear alone?"

Elias intervened. "Not by a danged sight! I'm the one who'll take care o' that grizzly. Webb, you will handle the lasso."

Webb spoke to Don Pasquel. "If one or both of us is alive, he or we are to be allowed to ride away tonight."

"Agreed," Don Pasquel said. "If Pablo Escobar could not do this, what chance do you *americanos* think you will have?"

"Bosh!" Elias snorted. "I'll show you how a real man goes about a little job like this. Your Pablo Escobar was so skeered he likely fainted when he got in there with that pig."

Don Pasquel bristled. "We will see how brave you are, my friend."

A new voice made itself heard. "This isn't fair. It isn't right. They shouldn't have to take a terrible risk like that."

It was Madge who was speaking. She was not far away. Webb discovered that she had been watching and listening from another window in a room nearby where she and Loa had been taken.

Don Pasquel bowed in that direction, then spoke to Webb. "The señorita intervened just in time. You must be grateful to her for seeing to it that —how is it you say it—your boast will not be called."

"If you want to call my boast, fetch out the items I asked for," Webb said.

Don Pasquel nodded grimly and gave orders that sent *mozos* racing to obey. Presently a sinewy, mouse-colored packhorse was led to the post. The pistols and rifle that had been taken from them were produced, along with another rifle that looked in fair shape.

"You will be provided with food too—if you are still able to ride away," Don Pasquel promised. "All of this is far more than the two of you are worth."

"And we'll really be allowed to ride away?" Webb insisted.

"That is the bargain," Don Pasquel said stiffly. "It is witnessed by all my friends. I have given my word."

"Fair enough," Webb said. "We're ready."

"There's nothing fair about it at all!" Madge called desperately. "Use some common sense. This is insane."

"Stay away from that window," Webb commanded. "Try and get some sleep."

"Sleep?" Loa echoed hysterically.

"Sleep, the man says," Madge gasped dismally. "Did you hear, Loa? We're to get some good sound sleep while this bloodletting is going on."

"All right," Webb growled. "Keep awake then. But stay away from that window."

Don Pasquel and his vaqueros unbolted the door and led Webb and Elias into the ranch yard. The onlookers stared at them wide-eyed, and many offered up prayers.

Don Pasquel offered the bullhide shield and knife that Pablo Escobar had used, along with the braided *reata* the smaller man owned.

Elias moved in to accept the knife and the shield, but Webb stepped up ahead of him and appropriated them.

"You handle the rope, Eli," he said.

He forestalled Elias's roar of indignation. "I'm depending on you to yank that bear around and keep him fighting the rope so as to give me an easy chance to move in on him. Those other two went at it wrong. The strongest should handle the rope, the fastest on his feet should handle the knife. Any fool ought to be able to see the sense of that."

"Blast you!" Elias groaned helplessly. "It sounds right, but it's wrong. You always was able to think faster'n me."

"I'd say you're both acting like idiots," Madge shouted from the window. "Stop this before it's too late! You saw what happened to that other poor man!"

Webb ignored her. He stripped off his jacket and shirt. Elias followed his example. A murmur ran through the onlookers as they gazed at Elias's mighty shoulders and muscle-plated chest. Along with his massive head and its tangle of thick, curling black hair, square-hewn features and rugged chin, he was as handsome as an Atlas.

"We all know you're a fine figure of a man," Webb said. "Quit posing for the señoritas and wasting time. See if you can hold this grizzly for me so I can sneak up on it."

They mounted to the parapet. Glancing back, Webb could see two faces at the window of the *casa* beneath the shadows of the *galeria*.

He moved along the catwalk. The grizzly, given respite from the attentions of the spectators, had been lying down. The appearance of these new opponents brought it to its feet with a snarl. It reared, growling, trying to make them out with its poor eyesight.

"He's a big one, sure enough," Elias said. He played out the loop through the honda. "I ain't exactly an expert with these here lassos, remember," he added. "See if you can pester him into watchin' you. Draw him off there to the left of me where I've got a chance to snag him."

Webb continued moving along the catwalk. He waved his arms and the bear fixed its attention on him. It dropped on all fours, moved across the arena, growling.

Rearing, it struck, trying to reach him with its claws. It fell short, but it tried again. Elias cast the loop at the right moment and the coil settled around the grizzly's neck.

Elias yanked the noose tight and caught the animal off balance, toppling it. The bear rolled to its feet in demonic fury, its teeth snapping as it fought to bite at the *reata*. Elias leaned back, the muscles bulging in his back. The noose tightened around the bear's throat.

Webb leaped from the parapet into the enclosure. His left arm was thrust through leather loops on the back of the bullhide shield. He held the shield in front of him as he landed on his feet. The long knife was in his right hand.

Up to that moment his plan had worked. Elias had snagged the bear and diverted its attention. The animal's vulnerable underside was exposed to the knife. But they were dealing not only with a wild beast, but one whose reactions were lightning-fast in spite of its clumsy appearance and whose strength was almost beyond belief.

And it was a huge animal. To Webb, it looked as big as the bull it had killed.

The bear saw Webb's leap. It whirled to face this nearer opponent, abandoning its attempt to fight the rope. It lashed out with a clubbing blow that seemed ponderous, but was catlike in its speed.

Webb had anticipated something like that and had darted back, holding the shield as a barrier. He did not escape entirely. The shield was torn from his arm. He was left facing the beast with only the knife as his defense. The bear reared again and came at him like a boxer, claws ready to disembowel him. He again leaped aside and once more escaped death, although the talons seemed to brush his shoulder.

He could not escape again. The bear seemed to fill all the world with its bulk as it reared above him. Then Elias found leverage for his moccasins and with a mighty heave on the rope again toppled the animal.

The bear's chest and belly were exposed. Webb leaped in, driving the knife home. The bear uttered a whining snarl of agony. Webb plunged the knife deep a second time.

He found himself flying through the air. His body struck the timbers. He had taken what amounted to a glancing blow from the grizzly's paw. He lay stunned.

The bear moved toward him. Elias toppled it

again. Then the *reata* broke. Blood was draining from the grizzly, but it moved again toward Webb. Elias leaped from the parapet, snatched the knife from Webb's numbed grasp and faced the animal.

The bear was weakening, but it came straight ahead, teeth bared. Elias side-stepped it, leaped on its back and leaned forward, driving the knife upward into its throat.

That ended it. The grizzly, dying on its feet, collapsed almost on top of Webb. He managed to roll clear before its full weight settled on him.

He got shakily to his feet. He and Elias stood panting, matted with blood and dust. Some of the blood was their own.

Webb discovered that the claw he had barely felt had done more than merely graze him. A gash had been torn in his upper arm. Elias was bleeding also, having been clawed on the thigh.

The trap gate was opened and they emerged into the ranch yard. The *fiesta* guests stood gazing at them in silence.

"Did you all get a good look at the slaughter?" Webb asked scornfully. "The bear was brave. He did not deserve to die. But it was better that he died fighting than to be tortured to death by people afraid to face him in the arena. There was no pleasure for us in killing him. It will be on our conscience."

Some of them understood English and he could

hear them translating what he had said. He expected an ugly reaction. To his surprise, they suddenly broke into applause.

"*Olé*! *Olé*! *Los americanos*!"

He and Elias looked at each other and shook their heads. "I'll never *sabe* these people," Webb said.

They moved through the crowd, walked to the fountain and dipped their arms in the cool water, splashing it over their bodies, washing away the dust and the blood.

"*Olé*! *Olé*!" spoke voices back of them. "*Los americanos*!"

Madge and Loa stood there, accompanied by Don Pasquel. She saw Webb's expression and said, "It's all right for us to cheer for our side too, isn't it? Yes, we watched the fight. You and Elias did well."

Webb searched around and found his shirt that he had discarded. It had been trampled by the guests as they had struggled for vantage points to watch the fight in the arena.

He started to rip a bandage from the shirt to bind his arm. Madge halted him. "It must have better care than that," she said angrily, reprovingly.

Loa turned on Don Pasquel and inundated him in a fiery flood of peremptory demands. Don Pasquel meekly ordered servants to bring bandages and medicines. A woman started to care for Webb's injury, but Madge motioned her aside. She and Loa took charge.

"Loa, tell the señora we've had considerable practice at patching up this man," she said. "He seems to be always getting himself involved with things like barnacles and bears."

Webb fumed with impatience while he endured the medication. "Hurry it up, can't you?" he demanded. "Raines . . .!"

Raines would be riding farther and farther away each minute. And there were many routes he might take, many ways by which he could blind his trail.

The instant Madge and Loa finished with the task, he and Elias pushed through the bystanders and strode toward the horses they had won. They halted, peering. Four saddled animals stood with the packhorse instead of two. The additions were sorrels that appeared to be fit and tough-muscled, but well gentled.

Webb whirled on Madge and Loa, suddenly guessing the answer. "What's this?" he demanded.

"We're going with you," Madge said.

"That's out of the question."

"Oh no it isn't. And you know exactly why we're going."

"But you don't know the *jornada*," he said. He saw that she was unyielding. "If we find what you want," he went on, "we'll bring it to you. That's a promise. We'll bring it to Goodhaven."

"It would be months at best before we ever heard of you two again," she said. "It would be years, more likely." She added, "And maybe never. Loa and I aren't ones to wait and worry. We would die."

She saw that Webb still meant to refuse. "Do you really believe that after what we've been through we're afraid of this *jornada* you talk about?" she demanded.

"It would at least be much better than being placed in prison," Don Pasquel spoke impatiently. "Soldiers are coming."

"Soldiers?" Webb exclaimed.

"They will be arriving in a few moments. They are from Monterey and are arresting all persons who are not citizens of Mexico."

"Are you telling the truth?"

"All *americanos* are being seized and their property confiscated. The governor gave the order several days ago, anticipating that war was coming. A messenger arrived a few minutes ago from the colonel commanding the detachment. He intends to bivouac his men here tonight."

"They wouldn't arrest women."

Don Pasquel shrugged. "The order includes all enemies of Mexico. Even the señoritas will be detained, I fear."

"Detained? Just what would that mean?"

"They will be taken to Monterey, or perhaps San Diego, until the governor has time to decide their cases."

"Would they be safe there?"

"Safe?" Loa exclaimed disdainfully. "In the hands of soldados? I would laugh if I were not crying."

"They probably would be sent to Mexico City," Don Pasquel said. He added, reluctantly, "There is much bitterness toward *americanos*. There has already been much trouble. And cruelty on both sides. I would not say that even the señoritas would receive the best of treatment. No, they would not be safe."

Webb stood frowning, at a loss. Madge spoke. "I can tell you which way Raines is heading."

Webb turned eagerly. "I'm listening."

She gave him a small smile, edged with frost. "We might even be able to overtake him before it's too late, provided we quit wasting time talking."

"So that's the club you're using. How did you get this information?"

"Bribery," she said.

"Bribery? With what?"

"The same sort of thing Raines used," she said. "Don Pasquel likes pretty stones."

Webb realized that the bargain had cost her the two pearls he had held out of the collection. He glared at Don Pasquel. "You thief!"

Don Pasquel flushed. "I am risking very much, señor!" he said. "*El coronel* will be very angry with me when he learns that I permitted *yanquis* to depart."

"Don Pasquel wouldn't let all four of us go just because you two killed a bear," Madge said. "He's more practical than that."

"Mercenary is the word," Webb said.

Elias lifted a hand for silence. "I hear sabers jinglin'!" he exclaimed. "Let's make tracks out of here an' talk this over some other time. Anythin's better'n a Mexican dungeon."

The sounds of the approach of a body of horsemen drifted from the darkness. Dogs were racing out, barking, to challenge them.

Webb glowered at Madge. "You've bought your way into more trouble, I'm afraid. All right. Let's move."

With Don Pasquel frantically pleading for haste, they made sure food had been provided and that the weapons had not been tampered with. Webb turned to help Madge into the saddle of one of the sorrels. He discovered that both of the sorrels were fitted with stock saddles. He had expected sidesaddles.

He began a question, but Madge said impatiently, "We asked for these saddles. Neither of us can ride well and we'll be better off this way. We're prepared for it. We've got the right kind of clothes —underneath. That was part of the bargain with Don Pasquel. We'll get rid of these skirts later on."

Loa spoke scornfully in Spanish to Don Pasquel as they mounted and wheeled the horses to ride.

"I tell him that I hope that *el coronel* makes him disgorge what my sister paid him for the *caballos* and the peon's clothes he sold us," she explained.

Two riders who had been waiting in the shadow of oak trees spurred out and joined them as they rode away.

Webb peered. "What's this?"

"This is Manuel Avila and his good wife, Chepita," Madge said. "They are going with us. Manuel knows the Spanish Trail. He will guide us. That's also a part of the bargain."

"At least you did your best to get your pearls' worth," Webb said. "Heaven preserve me from ever getting into a horse trade with you."

Manuel Avila was a leather-clad vaquero, small, wrinkled and with very high cheekbones and skin of deep coppery hue. It was his eyes that made him remarkable. They were fierce eyes, hawklike and very black.

His woman was also small and coppery, with the same hawk look. Like her husband, she wore a flat-crowned, wide-brimmed hat of a pale cream color that proclaimed them as mestizos of Spanish-Indian extraction. Although she wore a cotton skirt and petticoats, it was evident that she also rode astride in a stock saddle.

"We're gettin' neck-deep in womenfolk!" Elias snorted.

"She will be our duenna," Loa said haughtily.

"Duenna? Her?"

"You do not think we would be so shameless as to travel without a señora," Loa sniffed. "What a rogue you must be."

"In addition," Madge said, "Don Pasquel told us that Manuel has the sharpest eyes of any tracker in California."

"Tracker?" Webb exclaimed.

"Don Pasquel said Manuel will find and follow Raines's trail as easily as one rides down El Camino Real." She looked at Webb diffidently. "Yes, I fibbed a little. I don't actually know which way Raines is heading, but Manuel will find that out for us. Don Pasquel promised it."

"Or try to draw a knife across our gullets while we're asleep," Elias said sourly.

Loa talked to their new companions in Spanish. Their replies consisted mainly of "*No, señorita. Si, señorita.*"

"They are Yaqui mestizos," Loa explained.

"Yaqui?" Webb said. "The Yaquis hang out a long way from California."

Loa questioned them again. "They were captured when they were too little to remember and brought to California as slaves. But now they are free and are very grateful to Don Pasquel. They do not like *americanos*. That is all they wish to say, but they will obey Don Pasquel's orders to help us."

Looking back, Webb could see that the torchlit ranch yard was black with arrivals. The soldados.

They rode onward in silence and the torchlight faded into the darkness. Manuel led the way followed by Chepita on their wiry Spanish ponies. They set a steady, bone-jiggling canter. Webb and Elias, even though hardened to the saddle, disliked the racking gait. For Madge and Loa it was torture.

"Is my head still on top of my neck?" Madge finally moaned.

"Try to hold it still so I can get a good look at it," Webb said. "Yep. It's still there. It seems to be mighty loose, though."

Manuel did not look back or change the pace.

"How far is it—this *jornada*?" Loa asked plaintively.

There was no point in trying to conceal the truth from them. "It's up to a month's ride, with luck," Webb said.

"A month?" Madge groaned.

"It's around a thousand miles to Santa Fe, all told. But there are parts of it that are easy going, I've heard. Only the desert stretch is meant when they speak of the *jornada*."

"And how far is it across the desert?" Madge asked.

"That depends."

"On what?"

"On how much water you find and where you find it," Webb said reluctantly. "You first have to hit a river called the Mojave. But it's a river named the Virgin that holds the answer. If you can make it from one to the other you're out of the worst of it."

"How do you know this if you have never been there?" Loa asked.

"From trappers that both Eli and I have talked to. From the reports of Frémont and other men who've been over it."

None of them asked any more questions. They all knew they were heading, at the start of blazing summer, into a country where rivers that depended on the winter runoff from distant mountain snows might already be dry. There, each day's journey would be measured by the distance to the next water hole—a water hole whose existence was at the mercy of the unpredictable desert thunderstorms.

They rode on. Manuel, whose Yaqui brain seemed to be spelling out a trail in the darkness, whose Yaqui body apparently had the facility of gaining rest even at the jolting pace he set, gave them no mercy. The horses also seemed tireless.

It was past midnight, by the swing of the Big Dipper, when Webb saw that Madge was slumping limply in the saddle. She was clinging to the horn, too exhausted to lift her head but still too game to utter a complaint. Loa had been punished into the same sodden state.

"*Parar*!" he called. "Stop! We'll camp. The señoritas need rest. We all need rest."

Chapter Twelve

Manuel and Chepita reluctantly pulled up. Manuel located a camping site that offered shelter from the wind. Webb and Elias lifted the girls from the horses, for they were too numbed to dismount on their own strength.

"You'll get used to saddleback after a week or so," Elias said consolingly.

"A week?" Loa wailed. "I will be dead long before even another day. That four-legged *caballo demonio* is determined to kill me. It is pounding me into soft jelly."

They laid out tarps and blankets as a bed. "Spread yourself there, jelly-girl," Elias said.

They all slept until the first light of dawn. Manuel and Webb built a fire and Chepita began preparing breakfast.

Manuel spoke the first word he had uttered in the new day. "*Hola!*"

He was pointing to the black ashes of another campfire that had burned recently nearby. Webb tested the ashes with his hand and found them cold.

"Twelve hours," he said. "Maybe more."

There were many footprints around the fire. Some had been made by a man as big as Elias.

Jed Strapp. Manuel, by whatever magic was in his Yaqui mind, had placed them on the right trail. But Raines and Strapp had half a day's lead.

Don Pasquel had provided jerked beef and a bag of *penole*, which was ground parched corn mixed with brown sugar and cinnamon. Chepita braised strips of the stringy beef and fried cakes of *penole*, *tortilla*-style. There was coffee, shockingly strong, black and thick. It was standard trail fare in this part of the world.

"I'd give a purty to taste buffalo hump ribs again," Elias said as he chewed morosely on the tough jerky.

"You will shoot us this buffalo very soon now, eh?" Chepita asked hopefully.

"We're more likely to have jackrabbit an' lizards for grub," Elias growled. "I've heard men say they've never seen a buffalo west o' the Pecos River. An' that's a long way from here, I tell you now."

Loa waited, bright-eyed, expectantly. "What is this you are going to tell me?" she finally asked.

Elias glared at her. "I just got finished tellin' you," he said lamely.

Loa did not exactly understand, but she dutifully asked no more questions. Elias's mixture of jargon and sea terms was a puzzle to her. Also a fascination.

Webb and Elias saddled the horses while Chepita and Manuel broke camp. Webb paused, gazing as the girls came forward to mount. They were wearing the same type of rough, baggy blouses and cotton breeches that Don Pasquel had furnished himself and Elias.

"This is what I had in mind when I said we were equipped for riding stock saddles," Madge said. "We've stored the skirts on the packhorse."

"I can't say it adds anything to our elegance," Webb said, "but it might have one advantage. When Raines finds out we're on his trail, which he will sooner or later, he'll never guess that two of the party are females. He'll think the odds are even, and he never did like it that way."

It was Chepita, in her skirt and many petticoats, who had her nose in the air and patronized the two members of her sex who wore breeches.

The trail led them westward across the lush valley, passing by the mission church, which was deserted, the cultivated fields brown and weed-grown. At midafternoon they reached the olive-green mountains they had sighted from the west.

These proved to be rough, wild hills rather than mountains, matted with thickets of scrub oak and penetrated only by game trails. For two days they rode through this brushy labyrinth, following the tortuous meanderings of a drying creek whose channel offered the only feasible route for horsemen through this upended country.

On the third day they emerged into another valley. This was the great central valley—the San

Joaquin, so vast that the Sierra Nevadas, which walled it in to the east, were not visible.

A grass savanna rippled in a torrid wind beneath a blazing sun. It was a virgin valley, left untouched by the rancheros and the mission fathers who had found all the grass and land they needed in the more temperate areas near the coast.

They saw sign of elk and antelope, which evidently ranged this valley in great bands, but all wild game had vanished during the heat of the day to places of shelter or to broken hills that rose a few miles to the south.

There was no place to which a man or horse could turn for respite from the brassy glare. Saddle leather became too hot to touch with the bare hand. The wind parched lips and the mouth became cotton-dry. Manuel insisted that the water bags be used sparingly. It was evident that he was not sure of the distance to the next source of supply.

At dawn, Madge and Loa had been gay and rested, chattering in Javanese, which they knew offended Elias, for he suspected that he and Webb were the subject of their remarks and that they were being discussed and criticized without the pleasure of retaliation.

"It's not right to speak heathen words in a Christian land," he had thundered at them more than once.

They delighted in baiting him. And in annoying him by casual mention of exotic names and colorful places. Honshu, the Spice Islands, Molokai, Tongataboo. Places they evidently were as familiar with as yesterday.

But they were of the sea, and this land was alien to them and hostile. They wilted as the day advanced and Webb saw the spirit drain out of them in spite of their attempts to maintain a bold front. They were determined not to show the white feather. In them was the fear that Webb would send them back if they displayed any sign of weakening.

Manuel and Chepita seemed immune to hardship and heat. Or at least indifferent. The trail was easy to follow. Webb and Elias did not need Manuel's Yaqui skill, so plain were the tracks left by the passing of five men and six horses.

But always there was that gap between them—thirty miles, Elias and Webb estimated. The biggest part of a day's journey. On one occasion, as they were following higher country that overlooked great stretches of the ocean of grass through which they were passing, Webb believed he sighted their quarry far to the east.

But the heat waves moved in again, distorting all distant objects, and he was not sure but what he had seen was a mirage. Often a bush a pistol shot away would be magnified into the size of a tree. At other times a jagged outcrop of great boulders would be diminished until they could be mistaken for riders in single file far away.

At sundown they saw the dusty green tinge of willows in a draw—a promise of water. The horses quickened their slogging walk, the humans aroused.

There was water near the willows. The spot was little better than a swamp where an underground stream appeared briefly on the surface. But, as they rode nearer, a rancid odor of decaying flesh pervaded the air.

They pulled up and quieted the horses, holding the animals back as they sat looking at the water hole. The carcasses of four elk lay partly in the swamp, bloated and noxious and polluting the meager supply.

The animals evidently had been shot at dawn as they drank at the water hole. Meat had been taken for food from one elk, but the remainder of the kill had been left lying where the animals had fallen. The hot sun had done the rest.

Coyotes retreated as they rode nearer. Ravens and magpies arose with a thunder of flapping wings and circled complainingly. Flies and gnats swarmed.

"It tells us one thing at least," Webb said. "Sid wouldn't waste powder and lead without good reason. He's trying to make it tough on anybody who's following his trail."

"Do you suppose he knows—" Madge began.

"That we're following him. He can't be sure. But then again, maybe he sighted us at the same time I thought I might have spotted him. In that case, he *is* sure."

They dry-camped, staking the horses upwind from the water, and rationed what remained in the bags. Using Manuel's *reata*, they dragged the carcasses out of the swamp.

By noon the next day, the water hole had cleared and was safe for use again. They remained there for hours more, permitting the horses to recruit their strength. Then they filled the water bags and pushed on in the bitter heat of late afternoon.

Even so, Raines had gained another day's march by thus delaying them. Worse yet, if he had sighted them, there was now the danger of ambush—a factor that also was enormously in Raines's favor.

Webb rode in the lead, with Elias staying back. They carried rifles slung in their arms, primed and ready to fire. At intervals they changed places.

Trailing at a distance back of them came Madge and Loa, with Manuel and Chepita bringing up the rear. At times the cavalcade would halt while Webb and Elias scouted coulees or brush that might conceal a foe. Often, they veered far wide of points of suspicion.

No sign of danger appeared. The trail of Raines's party continued to lead them eastward, and now the lower reaches of the Sierra Nevada mountain chain began to lift slowly on the horizon —a sullen purple cloud. But always the threat of a trap was there, forcing them to plan and measure each mile of their advance, adding greater and greater strain on their nerves.

Manuel and his wife did not like this. At times, Manuel crossed himself. Chepita began fingering a rosary. They began to turn often and gaze longingly at their back trail.

A break began to emerge in the purple mountains ahead. "My guess is that's the pass Joseph Walker found hereabouts some years back," Webb said. "Frémont followed it too, a few years ago, using Walker's information, and hit the Spanish Trail in the Mojave Desert."

At twilight of a blazing day they reached water. It was a mountain stream, clear and sweet, which came from the gap that now loomed close at hand, breaking into the mountain wall.

They followed the stream into a canyon whose rims became increasingly higher as they advanced. The walls echoed back the hoofbeats of their horses.

Webb shot a young elk in a band they came upon in a meadow. The animals evidently had never learned to fear man, for they retreated only a short distance, then halted to graze again and watch curiously as Webb and Elias quartered the kill and placed the meat on the packhorse to cool.

Webb and Manuel selected a camp site on an

open sand bar as full darkness settled. They chose the spot as least likely to conceal rattlesnakes, for they had heard and seen the reptiles frequently since leaving the hot valley.

Webb ordered the three women to stay on their horses until he and Elias had rattled thickets near the sand bar and poked under boulders. The precaution was justified, for they routed out two snakes that slithered away, their rattles clicking. It was a sound as harsh and impersonal as this wild land around them.

Again Webb saw Chepita murmuring a prayer and Manuel standing with that uneasy fear in him.

They built a fire of manzanita twigs that formed a hot, small fire, hidden between flat rocks that they brought to the sand bar. An Indian fire. Madge and Chepita cooked elk steaks and elk liver and *penole tortillas.*

They ate in silence. Weighing on them was the knowledge that this was a place of final decision. Beyond this mountain pass was the desert and there would be no turning back. The hardships they had undergone were only a preliminary to what lay ahead.

Webb watched Madge as she worked over the cookfire, seeing that the others were provided for before she set aside her own portion. She had covered her hair with a turbanlike arrangement of cloth that gave protection from dust, with a flap that warded off the sun. The effect was oriental.

Loa, too, had put away the glitter shell comb and Spanish hair style in favor of a similar arrangement. She now seemed entirely oriental. The firelight played on her golden skin and seemed to find brooding kinship deep in her dark eyes.

At the moment, there was in her none of the vivacity and bravado that had carried her over these hard miles since the shipwreck. She sat cross-legged, partly in shadow, nibbling at her food.

Presently, Webb believed she was swaying a little and that her lips were moving. She was singing to herself. An almost inaudible song, with words in Javanese.

He realized it was not a song, but a chant. And she was dancing. Dancing mainly in her thoughts, with just the slightest swaying rhythm of her body to accompany the chant.

He did not even try to guess at what the words were saying or what her eyes were seeing. But her thoughts and her gaze were far away. She was not seeing the firelight into which she was looking, nor the dark mountains that frowned down on her. She had been transported some-where else. Far distant.

He discovered that this same mystic mood had reached Madge. She was dancing too, and joining in the chant, in silence also and with only the slightest swaying of her body.

Imagination had transported them back to some moment of beauty that they had shared together in the past and that they were sharing now in their thoughts.

The spell spread to them all. Elias and Manuel sat motionless, watching the two girls—and not seeing them. Their eyes were also brooding, laden with memories. Chepita sat as though turned to stone—a bronze image whose aspect was oriental also, in the play of firelight.

Webb thought of his brother. Suddenly, in his mind, he could plainly see Terry in his cell in prison. Terry had thinned and aged in three years. He was a caged animal—hopeless, frustrated. Deserted! That was it! Terry believed Webb had abandoned him. There was despair in his tortured face.

It was as though they were standing at arm's length, as though they were both there in the flesh. As though he was sharing Terry's inner emotions.

One thing was plain, above all. Terry would not live much longer in confinement. He was a man who had always been free. He was dying there—of broken wings—of a broken heart.

Webb came to his feet, staring wildly around, as though awakening from a dream. But it had not been a dream. He believed that completely. He had been with Terry for that moment. They had been brought together by some phenomenon he could not explain. It had not been sorcery, nor incantation. By prayers, perhaps.

His sudden movement had broken the spell. The others returned from whatever land to which their thoughts and hopes had carried them.

"What is it, boy?" Elias exclaimed, and grabbed hastily for his rifle.

"We've got to shove on!" Webb said hoarsely. "Now! Tonight! That new moon will be fat enough to give light until toward midnight before it sets."

He looked around at them, his voice rising. "Hustle! There's no time to lose!"

"What is it?" Madge asked.

"Terry will die," Webb said. "My brother. I just saw him—in prison. He can't live in a cage. He thinks I deserted him and—"

He broke off, realizing that it sounded crazy. But not to them, apparently. They understood! They asked no more questions. Madge and Loa leaped to their feet and frenziedly began breaking camp.

"Hurry!" Madge kept imploring. "Hurry!"

Webb halted them. He stood in front of them, grasping each by an arm. "You've got to go back," he said.

They froze into silence. "Manuel and his wife will go back with you," he said. "Anything's better than what's ahead."

All the energy, all the eagerness was draining out of them. They were suddenly spent, spiritless.

"We promised we'd fetch the pretty stones to you at Goodhaven if we got them," Webb said. "Remember?" His voice sounded hollow to him.

They didn't speak for a time. Madge finally said, "You'll be able to travel faster. We've slowed you down, haven't we?" She looked at Loa, who nodded despairingly. "We'll turn back," she added tiredly.

Manuel and Chepita had left the camp to saddle the horses, which they had picketed to graze on a flat above the stream some two hundred yards distant.

Webb, feeling that they had been gone overlong, seized up his rifle and went striding to find them. Reaching the flat, he scouted it, but saw no evidence of danger. The picketed horses seemed to be grazing at peace in the starlight.

"Manuel!" he called guardedly. "Chepita?"

There was no answer. He moved among the scattered horses, peering. There were only five animals in the flat. The mounts Manuel and his wife had been riding were missing. So were their saddles.

Webb returned to the camp, leading the remaining horses. "There're only four of us now," he said. "Manuel and Chepita have had enough of us. They've pulled out."

He saw the expressions on their faces. He

shrugged. "Can you blame them? They've been scared of us since the start. And praying all the way. And why not? Dead elk in a water hole, us prying at every spot on the way to make sure we weren't stepping into a dry-gulching. And chanting and praying."

"I'll ketch 'em an'—" Elias began.

"They've got a mile edge by this time, at least," Webb said. "We would only sull a horse and delay ourselves for days, trying to bring them back. There'd be no point in it."

He looked at the two girls. "Elias will go back with you," he said.

They stood gazing at him, and suddenly the life came back into them, the brassy spirit and vivacity.

"The nerve of him," Madge said scornfully. "Isn't he the bold, strong one, though. He's going ahead, but we are to go back where we'll be safe. He's going to pursue four able-bodied men singlehanded."

"He is very, very strong," Loa said. "He's the great hero who fought the duel with this savage, this Brass Kettle that you told me about. He is the one they named the *niños* after. He needs no help."

"You're hitting below the belt," Webb snarled.

"And you're treating us like children," Madge exclaimed. "Which, I assure you, we are not."

"I've noticed that," Webb said.

"We can't go back now, even if we wanted to, which we don't. Perhaps you've noticed that too."

"What about your reputations?" he asked. "There's no duenna now to look after you."

Madge said angrily, "Bosh! What reputations? After Chepita gets through with telling about us back at that rancho we'll be painted a brilliant red."

Loa gazed disdainfully down her nose at Webb. "This is now my duenna," she said. "It will protect the reputations of myself and my sister, I warn you." She patted the silver-handled Malayan kris, which she had placed in sight in the belt of her peon breeches.

Elias nudged Webb, grinning. "It's just like I told you about these slant-eyed ones. Make a wrong move an' you'll have that crooked knife between your ribs."

Webb looked at Madge. "And you? I suppose you've got the derringer?"

"I have," she said. "Then it's agreed that we're in this together."

"With a kris and a derringer at my throat, what can I say," Webb said. "It seems that we'll hang and rattle together."

"The hangin' might be the easiest part of it," Elias said. "We'll do a lot o' rattlin' on the *jornada*, that's for mighty certain."

Loa moved in, threw her arms around Webb and gave him a big, smacking kiss. "I, Loa Dolores

Djarak Martinique will tell you, señors, that we will not be a burden to you," she said happily. "It will be the other way, *si*. You will be the ones who will be glad of our strength, my brave *caballeros*."

They saddled and pulled out. They owed Manuel one debt. He had left them the pack animal.

They rode through the velvet blackness of the canyon, which veered so that they emerged into silvery moonlight. They moved through this white purity, the stream sighing softly nearby. A lark was awakened by the brightness and burst into song. Far away, another answered. Deep in the mountains, a wolf mournfully bayed the moon. Others joined in.

The night was sweet, the air soft and cool. It was a part of the spell that had fallen upon them when Loa and Madge had chanted their silent song.

It was a night to remember.

Two days later, they emerged at sundown from the mountains. Ahead, stretching to the horizon, lay a different country. A cruel country. The Mojave Desert.

Chapter Thirteen

Playas and dry washes glinted as white as bleached bones in the dying light of the day. Sterile mountain ridges squatted in shadowed sadness, brooding down on a land of thin, brittle brush, of alkali and wind-carved bluffs.

The long slant that sloped from their feet for miles to the desert proper was guarded by a weird army of deformed, thorned trees that some traveler in the past had said were the palms of Joshua. Gorilla-like in their shaggy coats, they spread crooked arms as though to enfold Webb and his companions.

Spanish dagger and deerhorn cactus presented their needle points. The fuzzy, yellowish glint of the villainous cholla showed among rocks and in crevices where it waited to numb the flesh of humans or animals with its millions of tiny barbs.

They pulled up and sat in silence, gazing. Webb looked at his companions. This land ahead, mailed in its armor and spikes, might be girded for battle and crouched to kill them, but there was some-thing dauntless and unswervable in the attitudes of the three who sat at his side.

Elias, ragged, his jaws black with the whiskers

that he kept under control by singeing with camp-fire brands, gazed at the desert, his chin thrust out challengingly. It was as though he was measuring the strength of an opponent and deciding how best to deal with him.

Madge and Loa had thinned still more, and were deeply tanned. More than ever, they could pass as young peons in their baggy garb. In them was a toughness of fiber and will that had astounded him. They too gazed at the Mojave in somewhat the same manner as Elias. Studying it, appraising its capacity to harm them, trying to decide how best to deal with its malevolence. In them was no terror.

They turned to him for instructions. That brought an uplifting emotion in him. They were one. The four of them were bound together in a cause where the chances of success were remote, the possibility of death very great.

He leaned from the saddle, placed an arm around Loa and hugged her. He turned and kissed Madge on the cheek.

"Why?" Madge asked, smiling.

"Because I'm glad you two came along," he said.

She looked at him, a deep glow in her, and they stirred the horses and rode ahead.

The trail of Raines and his party was still easy to follow. It pointed downward toward the desert. But the ashes of the last campfire they had made were more than twenty-four hours old. Raines was still gaining in the race. A little each day. But gaining.

Webb pointed. "Out there, somewhere, is the Mojave River."

"How far?" Loa asked.

Webb turned to Elias. "What would you say, Eli?"

Elias thought it over. "My guess is around three days," he said. " 'Bout a hundred miles, if I remember rightly what trappers told me about this country."

After a time, he added, "Findin' water in it might be tougher'n findin' the river."

"It seems that this river flows east for more than a hundred miles through the desert," Webb explained to the girls. "It ends up in a sink. From there the Spanish Trail winds among mountain ranges where there's water, and then follows a long, hard, dry *jornada* to the Virgin River."

Madge said, "Thank you."

"For what?" Webb asked, surprised.

"For beginning to treat us as equals." She added, "I say beginning. You haven't told us all the truth, even yet."

"Now, what—?"

"Raines is traveling faster than we are, isn't he? We're falling farther behind. Loa and I have slowed you down, haven't we?"

"No," Webb said. "That's where you're wrong.

We're setting our own pace. They're doing just what we want them to do. They're making too fast a trail. That could be fatal in this country. Look at it this way: Raines is the only horseman in the bunch, and the only one with experience at land travel. But he's running scared. The others don't realize what's ahead. All that will begin paying off, sooner or later. It will come down to whose horses are in the best shape. We'll stay with our knitting. We'll travel at night on the *jornada*, of course, spare our horses as much as possible and hope to wear them down."

"Maybe stickin' with our own knittin' is startin' to unravel them already!" Elias exclaimed. "Take a look!"

A rider had appeared far down the slope among the tree cactus. He had come off the desert. Webb set his horse in motion and they all rode to meet the stranger.

He was a dusty vaquero, a thinner and older replica of Manuel. He lifted his arm in a peace sign long before they came within rifleshot and sat awaiting them, apprehension evident in his manner.

"*Quiero ser su amigo!*" he kept shouting over and over.

"He wants to be very good friends with us," Loa said. "He is very dirty. He needs the bath."

The vaquero was not only dusty and grimy from travel and campfire smoke, but was bruised about the face and carried an arm in a sling made from strips torn from his blouse.

He talked to Loa. "He say he is the one Don Pasquel sent to guide the others," she explained. "He say he made the escape last night from those bad *americanos. Los americanos diablos*, he called them. Very bad. He say he tried to leave them days ago in these mountains, as Manuel and Chepita did, but they forced him to go with them into the desert. The man he calls *El Toro* broke his arm and beat him very cruelly."

"*El Toro*, the bull," Webb said. "That would be Strapp, of course."

"This man wishes only to go in peace back to Casa Molino," Loa said.

Webb gave the vaquero a portion of the *penole* and a chunk of meat and motioned him to ride on.

"Raines and Strapp are on their own now," he said, as he led the way toward the desert. "The same as we are."

Early darkness brought no relief from the stifling heat. It increased as they descended to the rough face of the desert, their way lighted by a bright moon.

Hours later, this changed abruptly. The desert became cold and brittle. A wind sprang up—the midnight mistral of the wastelands. It was a chill wind that carried sand in its teeth. They wrapped themselves in blankets and rode, bent and cowering and numbed with the cold. The horses tried continually to drift with the wind, but Webb and Elias forced the animals ahead. The North Star was their compass.

"They told me it was this way on this blasted desert at times," Elias mumbled. "A man boils an' stews under the sun in daytime. He roasts in early evenin' when the sand an' rocks let go o' their heat. But there's times like this one when he shivers, come mornin'. By daybreak he thinks he's goin' to freeze. Then the sun comes up an' you're in for another round of it."

They camped at dawn, with the moon setting and the morning star blazing. The wind had died.

Webb stood looking at a boulder, white in the growing light of daybreak. Written on the face of the rock with the black, charred ends of brands from a campfire was a message. It said:

"Don't be fools. We'll be waiting for you."

Like the dead elk in the water hole, it was a warning from Raines. This time the implication was plain. Raines knew they were trailing him. He was telling them they would walk into a trap and be killed if they kept going.

"They're gettin' spooky," Elias said.

"Good," Webb said. "They'll be traveling faster. Sulling their horses."

"Or maybe layin' in a bushwhack."

"Maybe," Webb said. "But I figure they'll wait to see if we make it across the desert. If they wanted a fight, they'd have tried it before this. Raines will try to avoid making a gun stand unless he's got a sure thing, or until he's cornered and can't get out of it. He's that kind."

"Not Strapp," Elias said. "He likes a fight. He's *that* kind."

"Strapp's only one in four," Webb said. "Biggle stacked up to me like a man who'd rather play it safe as long as possible, just like Raines. The sailor likely will do what Strapp and Biggle tell him to do. But Raines is the one who's calling the turn, not Strapp. He'll keep them running scared. But when Raines does turn to fight, he'll be a lot tougher than Strapp. Always remember that."

When they set out at sundown, they found that the easy trailing was over. Raines had split up his party. The four men had scattered in as many directions and had taken pains to follow rocky surfaces of hardpan where trailing was difficult.

"Greenhorn trick," Elias said scornfully. "It shows that Raines ain't thinkin' straight. They've got to get to the Mojave River. They'll join up there. There's no use in us wastin' time tryin' to spell out their tracks. We'll pick 'em up easier at the river."

They traveled all night across endless flats where only the inevitable creosote brush found foothold. They held a southeasterly course as best they could in a land broken by gaunt ridges and gulches. Occasionally, they skirted the flat white expanses of playas, or dry lakes. They were the sinks of streams or the remains of ancient lakes. Some of the playas actually were lakes in spring when the runoff from the great Sierra Nevada mountains to the northwest funneled down through the valleys and brought the lower desert to life. One or two showed the glint of water in their centers—alkali water. But the majority appeared to be dry and dead.

Some of these dry lakes stood across their route, offering inviting paths, flat as floors and entirely devoid even of the brittle saltbrush that grew in mounds around their rims. They longingly eyed these easy routes, but Elias insisted on skirting them. "Some likely are safe an' solid," he said. "But I've been told to stay clear of 'em all in this country. Some are mudholes with no bottoms. The top's baked white, like piecrust by the sun. But after a man an' a horse gets onto the cussed things, they break through. It's soft mud that swallows you. They say it's worse'n quicksand."

Hours later, in the cold hours before midnight, with the moon low in the sky and the icy wind beginning to moan, they were veering wide of one of these ghostly playas when they all pulled up their horses.

They sat listening. Terrible screaming drifted

faintly on the wind. The sounds came from a human and from a horse. Agonized sounds. The frantic outcries of a man and an animal who were being devoured alive by a monster.

Webb leaped from the saddle and raced among the mounds of saltbrush onto the margin of the playa whose white expanse gleamed in the moonlight.

Far out on the surface was a formless, dark shape, tiny at that distance. It was from there that the screaming came.

Elias, pursuing him, overtook him and wrapped arms around him, bringing him to a stop. And none too soon, for he could already feel the rubbery, queasy movement of the surface beneath their feet.

It was slowly buckling. Even here, the playa was a death trap. The man who had ridden so far out must have been unfortunate enough to have found firmer footing for a distance into the sink until it was too late to turn back.

"You'd only go under too!" Elias panted. "There's nothin' we can do. There's nothin' anybody can do."

It was already over. There was no sound now on the wind. The surface of the playa once again lay unbroken and flat, shining coldly in the moonlight. The dark shape had vanished.

They turned in terror and ran to escape from this silent monster. Reaching the horses, they mounted and headed away. They all rode for a long time without speaking.

"Which one?" Madge finally asked.

"No telling," Webb said. "My guess is that it was the seaman. Or maybe Biggle."

"How long had—had he—?" She shuddered and couldn't finish it.

Webb hesitated. "Not long. He probably lost direction and traveled in a circle for a day." But both he and Elias were inwardly sure the man had been trapped for hours, fighting vainly to escape.

"Why the sailor or Biggle?" Madge asked. "Why not Strapp? Or Raines?"

"Biggle and the sailor would be the ones most likely to get into trouble traveling alone on the desert," Webb said. "I doubt if Strapp would let Raines get very far away from him as long as Raines is carrying the pretty stones. Biggle and the sailor were left to look out for themselves."

"Raines likely forgot to mention to them that there was such things as sinkholes that could swallow them," Elias said. "It makes one less to reckon with when they divide up the stones."

In the blazing heat of noon the following day, after a march that started the previous sundown, they reached the Mojave River. Or its course, rather. They sat staring with sinking hearts. The wide bed of the stream, fringed with willow and mesquite, was only an expanse of dry sand.

"It's an upside-down river," Webb said. "It runs underground in summer, most of the distance, but it shows on the surface in places."

They followed the bed of this strange, dry river. It was midafternoon before they found water on the surface. By that time their tongues were swelling in their parched mouths.

Water revived both humans and animals. They camped in the shade of honey mesquite trees that gave respite from the weight of the sun.

It was a cheerless place of half-stagnant water, dusty brush and insects. A place of both life and death, for the weaker creatures of the desert that came here to drink were prey for the stronger. The struggle for existence was written in the pawprints and in the gnawed bones, some of them not many hours old.

However, the horses found nourishing forage in this desolate spot in the mesquite pods that littered the soil. They visibly strengthened and regained their spirit as they filled on food and water.

For the humans there was only the cooked, stringy flesh of a jackrabbit that Elias had shot and the *penole*, which they were treasuring as though its grains were gold.

Madge and Loa fell almost instantly asleep on blankets spread in the shade of the mesquite. They lay with their heads cradled on their arms, their faces and eyes turned to the earth and away from the glare of a sky that was becoming intolerable to them. They talked and mumbled and sometimes sobbed in their dreams. For it was only in their sleep that they gave voice to the fear of death that was in them.

Webb looked down at them and then at Elias. There was agony in his eyes. Self-accusation. "If either of them die, it'll be me that killed them," he said. "I should never have let them come into this hellhole."

"No power on earth could have stopped 'em," Elias said. "They're happy."

"Happy? In this purgatory? How can you say that?"

"You're happy too, Webb. Not the kind of laughin' happy. The other kind. That goes deep. The kind of happy a man—or a woman—has inside him when he's faced up with rough doin's, an' he does what he has to do. You wouldn't want to be any other place in the world than right where you are now. You're not doin' this for yourself. Nor for the price of the purty stones. They don't mean anything to you. Not any more. Nor to them. You might have coveted them once. I know I did. I admit it. But that's over with. It's Terry you're thinkin' about. An' it's for the people of Goodhaven that those two are goin' through this furnace."

Elias looked down at the sleeping Loa. His voice softened. "As for that one, there's another reason she's here. Her an' her slant eyes. Her an' her heathen dancin' an' prayin' to heathen gods. Oh, yes, I've seen her pray."

Webb had seen Loa praying also, bowing to the east and humbling herself to some unseen presence. She had always tried to be alone during her worship, but that had often been impossible. Her prayers had been completely sincere, unaffectedly simple and evidently richly sustaining, for she had always risen refreshed and strengthened.

"God forgive me for considerin' myself above her," Elias said, his voice husky. "She's loyal. She's in this because the other one is. They're sisters, closer together than ties of blood. They've faced death together. One would never desert the other."

He looked at Webb. "An' they'd never desert us, no matter what it cost them."

"Nor would you desert them," Webb said. "Or me."

"I wasn't talkin' about me," Elias mumbled, suddenly embarrassed by his display of emotion.

Webb slapped him on the shoulder. Together they walked out to move the picket pins so the horses could reach fresh grazing.

Chapter Fourteen

They were on foot, leading the horses. The Mojave Desert and its phantom mountains were days behind them now. The cheerless camps they had made on its water holes were memories of paradise, for this high desert that they traveled was their real purgatory. Each footstep was exactly like the previous effort, each mile like the one that had just been conquered.

The hot, loose soil burned through their thin footgear. The horses walked mechanically, heads drooping. They were too exhausted to carry riders.

Mountains stood to the east and to the west— as arid and harsh as the mesa over which they traveled. The creosote brush was stunted and thinly spread, each shrub clinging to its hummock of hot, dry earth.

This was the *jornada.* The trail of Raines and his party led across this vast, hot mesa also, but the tracks were wind-blown and old. At least three days old. They had picked up that trail on the Mojave River at a point where Raines had evidently arranged a rendezvous. From the footprints they had found they had decided that it was Biggle who was still with Raines and Strapp, and that it had been the seaman who had died in the sink, as Webb had surmised.

Webb had insisted on camping for two days in a mountain meadow they had reached after emerging from the sink of the Mojave River. Two days' delay had given Raines that much more advantage over them, but Webb had forced them to rest there where the horses had grass and water before moving into the last dry march.

Even so, they were afoot, and the horses were gaunt and would not last many hours longer without water. But the Virgin River could now be no more than a few miles ahead, if their estimates were correct.

Not only the horses were failing; Elias suddenly lifted Loa in his arms and carried her. She had started to stumble blindly.

"You don't weigh much more'n a mountain quail," he said from dry, heat-cracked lips. "An' you're just as soft an' downy."

"How strong you are, my brave one," she sighed. "But I will not have this. You will put me down." She tried to smile at him—and succeeded. "But not for another little minute," she murmured. "It is nice here. Very, very nice."

Webb looked at Madge and placed an arm around her to help her. She shook her head and moved away. "Let me keep going on my own feet as long as I can," she said. She added grimly, "We'll make it! We've got to."

"We will make it," Loa echoed. Then she promptly fell into exhausted sleep in Elias's arms. He continued to carry her.

They topped another of the endless swells in the dry plain. Carrion birds rose ahead from the carcass of a dead horse. Little more than the bones remained, for the animal had been dead some two days by the indications. It had died still bearing its saddle, and the coyotes had destroyed even this.

"Big horse," Elias said. "As big as the one Don Pasquel gave me. It must have been Strapp's."

They trailed on past, and the crows and magpies settled back to resume their squabbling.

Scarcely more than a mile farther on they came upon a spectacle even more grim. This time it was a man who had been left to the birds and coyotes.

Webb and Elias left the girls at a distance and walked closer. "Biggle," Webb said. "They're the bones of a man smaller than even Raines."

The story was plain enough. It was Strapp's horse that had died, but it was Biggle who had been set afoot. Strapp and Raines had abandoned him. He evidently had tried to follow them, but had wandered in a dementia of thirst. Here he had fallen and died, apparently having started to turn back, his fevered mind tricking him, no doubt, in trying to make it back to the sea.

They covered what was left with rocks, but

these were small and inadequate. As they pushed on, they could hear the flutter of wings and the squawking once again.

At sundown, an eternity later, the ears of the horses lifted and from them came little excited sounds, almost childlike in their pathos.

Webb and his companions caught the fragrance at the same time. The hot wind brought the sweetness of water—a perfume that maddened them. They let the animals run free. They, too, stumbled frenziedly ahead in a race toward this source of life.

They had reached the Virgin River! They had emerged from purgatory! The *jornada* was behind them!

They stumbled into the river and splashed like maniacs, letting life and hope drain back into their parched bodies.

They were still laughing and wild with the miracle of it, the miracle of being alive, when they emerged, their ragged clothes clinging to them.

They sobered and quieted, staring at the ashes of a campfire that had been used no more than a few hours ago, for, when Webb tested it, he found brands still with life in them.

Raines and Strapp had camped here for at least two days, by the signs. They had been forced to rest their horses after the ordeal of the *jornada*.

"We'll be on their heels before another sundown," Elias said. "They're just about afoot already. Their animals will need more rest than this. Horses don't come back in a hurry from what theirs has been put through."

Webb bent to study the footprints around the site of the fire. That movement saved his life. A rifle bullet that might have torn through his brain only grazed his hair and slapped into the earth with a savage impact.

He and Elias had been under fire enough times to know the best procedure. They moved fast. Webb scooped up Madge, who was kneeling, arranging her soaked hair, and dove with her to the shelter of a sizable boulder.

Elias snatched Loa off her feet. Nearest cover for him was offered by the trunks of small mesquite trees, back of which he darted. A bullet tore a furrow in one of the trees near his head. He dropped to the ground with Loa in his arms and rolled toward better shelter of boulders a dozen yards away.

Webb left Madge and dove into the open, snatching up his rifle. He saw the flash of the second shot. The rifleman was hidden on the rocky lip of a bluff across the river. The stream at this point curved against the base of the abutment, which rose some fifty or sixty feet to a brushy rim.

It would be Raines who was doing the shooting. That was the thought in Webb's mind as he crouched there, lifting his rifle. Raines had a reputation as an expert marksman, but he had again missed Elias, who was still his target.

Raines had emptied two rifles. There had been no weapon beside Biggle's skeleton, which meant that Raines probably had a third rifle available and loaded.

Elias, who was still rolling with Loa toward the boulders, would again be the target, for Raines was not likely to throw away a better chance by trying to swing his sights on Webb in that split second.

Webb fired. He had only the most general idea of Raines's position on the bluff. But he knew Raines, knew the value the handsome man placed on his skin. He fired only to upset Raines's aim.

He succeeded. A third wink of powder flame came from the rim. Webb heard the bullet strike solidly nearby. But Raines had missed Elias and Loa again. The slug had buried in the earth. In the next moment Elias had reached safer shelter along with Loa. Webb raced back to cover, crouching alongside Madge.

"Stay down!" he warned.

Silence came and held for a time. Then a shot echoed from the bluff.

Madge uttered a little moan. "Oh, no!"

Webb restrained her attempt to rise. The bullet had struck one of their horses as it stood knee-deep in the river with its companions. The animal's legs crumpled and it sank tiredly into the river, as though finding rest and peace at last from men and their ways.

Webb frantically raced to where his powder horn and the shot pouch lay, risking a bullet. He got back to shelter unharmed and frantically began reloading his rifle. But Raines had easier targets. He fired a second shot. And another horse was hit.

"Stop it!" Madge screamed. "Stop it!"

The answer was a third shot, killing another animal. This was fired from a different point, to which Raines had moved.

The fourth horse died only after the interval needed for Strapp to finish reloading the first rifle and hand it to Raines. Then came the turn of the packhorse.

Madge and Loa lay sobbing. The animals had shared their hardships with patience. Their reward had been death.

Raines never spoke, but Strapp could not help taunting them. "That's just to keep Sid in practice. You fools will be next on the list."

Elias lifted his voice. "You're my size, Strapp. You're yellow if you don't give me a chance to bust you across my knee."

Strapp, proud of his physical prowess, rose to the bait. "I'll see that you get the chance," he yelled.

"There's no better time than now," Elias answered.

Strapp evidently was of a mind to take up the challenge, but Webb heard Raines talking angrily. Silence came.

"How about it?" Elias yelled jeeringly.

There was no answer. Webb cautiously poked his head into view, trying to draw a shot. None came. Finally, he emerged entirely from shelter. The bluff was deserted.

"Raines talked Strapp out of it," he said. "They've pulled out."

Dusk was settling. He walked to where the horses lay in the margin of the river. Two were still alive but beyond help. He put them out of their suffering with his pistol. It was better than leaving them to the magpies and the wolves.

He stood for a space before turning away. "Don Pasquel raises good horseflesh," he said. "I wonder where faithful animals go when they die."

Chapter Fifteen

They were burdened only by their weapons and the scant camp packs that Elias and Webb shared. They had salvaged from the saddles a *reata*, the maguey picket lines and the cinches and latigo straps, for ahead of them lay a country of canyons and swift rivers where crossings might be dangerous and ropes would come in handy.

They followed the Virgin River for three days through rugged, broken country. This led them to higher, cooler valleys where the scrub cedar gave way to pine trees, where streams emerged from mountain draws and fat mule deer were plentiful. They strengthened on venison.

Strapp and Raines were still following the Spanish Trail, which was a vague trace that only trappers and Santa Fe traders traveled at long intervals with their pack trains. Their horses evidently had benefitted by the rest on the Virgin. Raines and his companion were again more than a day's journey ahead and adding to their advantage each day.

But, inevitably, Raines would attempt another ambush. Webb was certain of that. Therefore he and Elias avoided the trail itself, preferring to find their own way through the mountains into the next watershed, which would be the valley of the Sevier River.

It was late afternoon when they followed a small stream out of timbered mountains in which they had been struggling for days and came in sight of a green valley, threaded by a sizable stream.

Webb, who was leading the way, suddenly crouched down and motioned to the others to halt. Elias came crawling to join him.

"That must be the Sevier," Webb said. "But take a look at what we've got."

An Indian camp stood in a meadow alongside the stream no more than half a mile away. Ponies grazed under guard. There were more than a hundred animals in the *remuda*, although Webb doubted if there were a score of Indians in the camp. No lodges had been set up and there were no women or children in the party. Lances were thrust in the ground and the tribesmen were squatted about small fires, eating.

Madge and Loa came crawling to their side. "Stay down," Webb warned. "I don't want them to spot us—not yet."

"Plenty of ponies," Elias muttered longingly. "They ain't Paiutes. Nor Utes."

"They're Navajos," Webb said.

"Danged if you ain't right," Elias said. "I've seen some of 'em at Taos at times. Now what are they doin' in these parts? They belong on the other side o' the big canyon."

"Raiding party," Webb said. "Heading home after stealing horses from the Utes or Paiutes."

"*Los caballos*!" Loa breathed excitedly. "What I would give for one to ride."

"Seems like I recollect you singin' a different tune about horsebackin' not so long ago," Elias commented.

"It is now my poor feet that I sing the tune about," she said loftily. "They are one big hurt. Before that, it was—"

"Let's not go into that," Madge spoke hastily.

Webb speculatively eyed the derringer Madge had in her belt, and the silver-handled kris that Loa carried. But, most of all, he appraised the shell glitter comb that Loa had taken to wearing in her hair for want of a safer place.

"Just what would you give to ride a horse again, Loa?" he asked. "Maybe we could do some trading with these Indians."

Loa spoke in a small voice. "The kris, yes. It means nothing to me. But my *peineta*? It is only a pretty ornament. It would not be worth a *caballo*."

"It might be worth more than a horse to them. They like pretty ornaments. We need horses. Four at least, but most of all we need to find a short trail across the canyon country. The derringer should buy a good pony. The kris might likely appeal even more to them. I doubt if they've ever seen a knife like that. And we could spare a pistol."

"But not our scalps," Elias said. "You don't aim to go down there an' dicker with 'em face to face, do you?"

"That's the only way it can be done. These fellows must have come from the north or from west of here and are heading back to Navajo country. The Spanish Trail loops a long way north to avoid the canyons along the Rio Colorado. It swings a hundred miles or more out of a straight line to Santa Fe. That means that these Navajos must know a short trail across the canyons east of here. If we could cut off that big swing north, we'd save a week's travel."

They came to eager attention. "We might even get ahead of Raines and Strapp," Webb added.

"An' be waitin' for 'em to come along, instead o' them alayin' for us," Elias breathed. "Now, wouldn't that be a jolt to Sid Raines! An' to Strapp!"

Webb arose to his feet. "Fetch your rifle, Eli," he said. "Stay back of me, and hold off at gun-shot distance while I go in and palaver with them. That'll let them know that at least one of them will go under with me if they jump me."

He handed his pistol to Madge. "On second thought," he said, "we'd probably get a better horse for my rifle than the six-shooter. And you might have need for the pistol."

The girls knew what he meant. They were not to let themselves be taken alive, if it came to that.

"Be very, very careful, *querido mio*," Loa said huskily. "If you die, I think me and my sister will wish to die too."

"Nonsense," Webb said. "I don't aim to die. I've held peace powwows with Comanches when they were painted. And Kiowas. Navajos can't be any tougher to deal with than those tribes. Indians usually respect the palaver sign."

Loa handed him the kris. Then she removed the comb from her hair. She fondled it a moment, put it to her lips, then handed it to him. "It will protect you," she said. "My mother will watch over you. The comb, it brings good luck."

"Your mother? This was your mother's comb?"

It was Madge who answered. "Yes. It's all that Loa has to remember her by. But her mother would want it this way. Maybe that's why Loa's been able to keep the comb for so long. Maybe it will do what you say."

She handed him the derringer. "But if it doesn't, this gun is loaded. It might save you much—much pain."

She suddenly was in his arms. She wanted to weep, but she fought that off. She kissed him, and her tears stained his unshaven face. "My dear!" she choked. "Oh, my dear!"

"No bullet could kill me now," Webb told her. "No arrow. No lance."

He kissed her again and disengaged her arms. "Let's go!" he said to Elias.

"*Vaya con Dios*!" Loa breathed.

Madge echoed it. "Go with God!"

Webb walked into the open and headed toward the Indian camp. He was sighted at once. Warriors sprang to their feet, lifting muskets and bows. Their excitement increased when Elias appeared.

Elias halted within easy shot of the camp, his rifle cocked and slung in his arm. Webb lifted his own rifle, pointing it into the sky, and fired it. He continued on toward the Navajos with the empty weapon, his arms extended to show that he had no other gun.

The warriors quieted and waited. They were stocky men who wore goatskin shirts and breeches of tanned sheepskin, with leggings to the knee and beaded headbands to control their coarse, black hair. They had necklaces and arm bands of silver and polished copper. There was a savage and arrogant pride in them.

Webb walked among them. He spoke in English. "Does anyone speak my language?"

For a time they only gazed at him scornfully. At last one spoke in a mixture of English, Spanish and Navajo, along with sign language.

Webb drew from his pocket the derringer. He discharged both barrels in the air. The warriors were startled in spite of themselves.

He placed the derringer at his feet. He pointed to the pony herd, singling out a solid bay that appeared to have the makings of a good saddle mount.

"I will trade," he said.

They all understood that. The leader of the Navajos, a muscular man of powerful features and graying hair, proved that he was no novice at the fine art of bargaining, for he pretended to disdain the offering, refusing even to look down at it. Yet Webb knew that he coveted it. He probably had never seen such a weapon.

He also proved that he knew how to say no, for he uttered the word now with vast contempt.

Webb shrugged and picked up the derringer. Pocketing it, he started to turn away. The chief spoke a word, halting him. Webb turned, gazing inquiringly. The chief made a gesture and a warrior ran to the pony herd and presently led in a scrawny beast that was the poorest of the lot.

The chief tried to place the leather hackamore rope in Webb's hand. It was Webb's turn to become scornful. He walked around the animal, laughing jeeringly. He made signs indicating that this beast was too old to be of any use except to feed to the coyotes. He patted the derringer and pointed to a second horse of greater quality. The derringer, he told them with gestures, was worth two such worthless beasts. But this other one, this crowbait. He would not give a pinch of sand for it.

All Indians loved to dicker. The chief, always

aware that Elias stood ready to pick him off, ranted and raved. He threatened Webb with his rifle, but it was only sound and fury and both of them knew it.

The bargain was finally closed. One pony for the derringer. And the pony was the bay Webb had originally picked.

Webb next produced the kris. That brought a murmur of wonder. He saw the glint in the eyes of the Navajos. Artisans themselves in working metal and polishing stones of the desert, they recognized craftsmanship.

The kris was good for two more ponies, but the haggling and the threatening went on for nearly an hour and twilight was at hand before the two hackamore ropes were placed in Webb's hand and the chief picked up the kris.

Webb's rifle brought another pony, and that seemed to be standard price, for there was little dickering on either side.

He stood with the hackamore lines of four ponies in his hand, and began the final and most important bargaining of all—the attempt to have the Navajos agree to lead them across the area of the great canyons.

When the Indians finally understood Webb's request, they burst into a savage chorus of refusal. They did not want their trails to become known to anyone outside their nation, particularly a member of his race.

Webb produced the shell comb, holding it so that its brilliants glittered in the last reflection of the sun from the sky. That brought silence. The Navajos began to crowd in, desire for this trophy in their eyes. And also there was anger in them at the audacity of the white man for placing this temptation before them.

They might have forgotten Elias, but he raised a warning shout. That brought them back to reality and they drew back. Webb began breathing again. He had never been nearer to death, and knew it.

The Navajo chief offered a pony for the comb. Two ponies. Three. He kept saying, *"Santa Fe. Señorita!"*

Webb guessed that he had been to Santa Fe and had seen such combs in the hair of Spanish beauties. Evidently he or his wife had always desired to own such a thing.

Abruptly, temptation overcame caution. The chief nodded angrily. The bargain was made. The comb changed hands.

Webb turned and shouted. Loa and Madge appeared and he motioned them to come into the Indian camp at once, for he did not want to give the Navajos time to change their minds. Once they were all guests in the camp, they likely would be reasonably safe under the code of hospitality among primitive people. What might come later, after they parted, was another matter.

Madge and Loa joined Elias and came hurrying to Webb's side. The Navajos covered their mouths in amazement when they realized that the two slender persons were women. And, above all, white women in masculine garb.

One warrior fingered Loa's hair. She gave him a resounding slap. He backed away, dumfounded. A cackle of laughter arose from the other Navajos. That eased the situation. They were accepted as guests. They were even offered food. Webb tested it and said that it was venison, although to tell the truth he wasn't sure. But Madge and Loa had faith in him and ate confidently.

The comb and the kris and derringer were on display. Soon, the Navajos were shaking dice for the trophies. It was a tense gambling game, with the prizes so big that it came to the point of bloodshed at times, with warriors drawing knives.

The uproar and the squabbling went on until late in the glare of campfires. Elias watched this with growing scorn. "If the Utes or Paiutes was trailin' these fools to get their horses back, they'd never have a better chance than right now," he said. "They've forgot about everything except tryin' to win them gewgaws." But no foes appeared.

At last the camp quieted. The winners of the treasures pranced around for a time, boasting and taunting the unlucky ones. Finally, they too rolled up in their blankets.

Madge and Loa slept. Webb and Elias took turns standing guard over them and the horses they had acquired.

When morning came, they set out with the Indians, riding well back of them, watchful for treachery. But though some of the younger of the warriors would at times upbraid them and make mock charges at them, brandishing knives and lances in their faces in an attempt to make them flinch, the code that protected guests prevailed.

They traveled for three days through a maze of stupendous canyons and soaring cliffs. They followed trails that clung to the faces of precipices and carried them into gloomy gorges where dark streams thundered and giant ferns brushed their faces. Here the tiger lily bloomed.

They descended a long gorge and forded a wide and savage river, so laden with silt it was almost a thing alive, a red-brown serpent writhing through the canyons.

"Rio Colorado!" the Navajo chief said.

A hard day's ride brought them to higher country—the mesa country of the Navajos. Here they parted with their hostile hosts.

The parting was abrupt. The Navajos merely swung south. When Webb and his companions started to follow, not realizing that the Indians considered their agreement fulfilled, the chief raised a rifle and fired a ball close over their heads.

Webb and Elias sat ready to use their pistols and their remaining rifle in case an attack was coming, but the Navajos rode away, whooping their opinion of them, and vanished into the wildness of the region, leaving them to shift for themselves.

Around them was a vast land that had been colored by a vivid and lavish brush. A land of stone and sand and sky, carved into fantastic formations. Fat, white clouds floated in a sapphire sky.

Webb and Elias dismounted and squatted down, drawing finger maps in the soil, jig-sawing together what they could remember of the geography of the region from descriptions they had listened to and charts they had looked at in the past.

"I'd say we're less than two days' ride south of where the Spanish Trail fords the Rio Colorado after it starts its swing south toward the Santa Fe country," Elias said. "I've been told that beyond that ford there's a place where the rocks are all bent in circles."

Webb continued to squint at their map, making thumb and finger estimates of distance. He designated a place with his forefinger. "This is the Green River ford," he said. "It's a good day's trip west of the Colorado ford. My guess is that they're nearing the Green by this time. But their horses will be sulled, and they'll likely have to lay over there for a day or two."

He looked up at the girls. "If we're guessing right, we can be waiting for them when they ford the Colorado," he added.

They mounted in a sudden frenzy of haste and headed north. They soon came back to sanity and slowed the pace, but Webb could see the fierce fires burning in them. In him was the same wild hunger.

Behind them was the Mojave Desert and the *jornada.* Farther back, but still sharp in memory, were the crossing of the San Joaquin Valley, the fight with the grizzly, the shipwreck. And for Webb there was the recollection of those three years in exile, three years of Terry waiting in a cell.

Now, for the first time, he felt that he and Elias might have gained a real advantage.

They swung far east of the Rio Colorado, which remained buried in its gloomy canyons, so as to skirt side streams that also burrowed deep beneath the surface of the land.

They came upon an Indian trail and this helped them find feasible routes around or through the defiles, but the two days that they had estimated to the ford of the big river lengthened to three. And then to four.

The eagerness drained out of them, and hope faded. Because of the maddening obstacles the country placed across their path, the chances now were that Raines and Strapp would have forded the Colorado by this time and be east of them, heading into the main range of the Rocky Mountains where they would have a choice of many ways to shake off pursuit for good.

It was late on the fourth day when they stood in the stirrups, galvanized by the sight of water far ahead glinting in the lowering sun.

"The river," Webb said.

Here the Rio Colorado emerged from the depths and ran as a river should, strong and flat on the surface of God's earth. Here, it was a river, and not a creature of the tombs.

Far beyond the river stood what seemed to be the ruins of an ancient city. Stone arches, miniature at that distance, were sharply defined to the eye in that crystal air. Structures with graceful spirals stood in the sun, silent and eternal.

But these ruins were more ancient than any city. It was a world of stone, a world where stone had been bent into circles. A land of giant arches formed by the elements through the ages.

They rode ahead. Suddenly, Elias drew a long sigh. "See it!" he said, speaking in a hushed voice as though fearing to frighten away that at which he was pointing.

Webb saw it also, but Madge and Loa, inexperienced at such things, were unable to mark out the blue of smoke against the blue of these skies at that distance. They only stared blankly.

But it *was* smoke! The smoke of a campfire!

Chapter Sixteen

"It's on this side of the river," Webb said, and he was using that same subdued tone. "If it's them, they've forded and have camped on this side. I see green graze along the river."

They rode toward the beacon, staying below the swells and outcrops so that their approach would not be discovered. The sun was in their eyes. Presently, it was gone, leaving a golden lacework along the saw-tooth rims of the mountains to the west.

Elias, who had urged his pony into the lead, suddenly rammed back in the saddle, yanking his mount to a halt. The others pulled up.

Across their path lay a deep arroyo. It was, in fact, a small canyon. The wall at their feet dropped almost sheer to a small stream. It was a drop of nearly a hundred feet. The distance to the opposite wall was little more than an easy pistol shot, and that wall was terraced, rising in easy steps of stratified rock.

It was characteristic of this land that there had been no evidence of the obstacle until they were at its brink. And it *was* an obstacle. Webb and Elias scouted for a mile in opposite directions and returned tight-lipped.

"This danged gulch seems to keep goin' for quite a spell east o' here," Elias said. "It might peter out toward them ridges you kin see, but it'd be long past dark before we could make it that far."

"It cuts deeper as it swings to join the river in the other direction," Webb said. "There's no easy crossing." He gazed at the sky. The streamer of smoke had vanished.

"We could lose a day trying to find a way around it," he said. This new frustration was like a sickness on them.

He moved along the rim and found a place where a rockfall lay against the base of the cliff. He estimated that the sheer drop here was no more than sixty feet to the rocks. Tough scrub cedar grew near the rim, close at hand.

He raced back to the horses. "We can reach bottom with the *reata* and the picket lines," he said.

"Then what?" Elias asked.

"That other flank can be climbed without much trouble. You can lower me and I'll scout that camp. It might not be made by the ones we want. If so, we're wasting valuable time and should be heading east. We've got to know."

None of them relished his proposal. "You won't do anything foolish?" Madge asked anxiously.

"Foolish?"

Elias answered that. "Like jumpin' 'em singlehanded, if they turn out to be the right ones."

Webb considered that. "No," he finally said. "I wouldn't want to throw it away, not after waiting three years. I'll play it safe."

"Safe?" Madge echoed drearily, gazing into the gorge where dusk was gathering and the stream whispered sullenly.

"He will play it safe," Loa said. "Again, it is to laugh if I were not weeping."

They lashed picket lines to the *reata* and the combined line easily reached the rockfall. Elias took a turn of the rope around a cedar, using the tree as a snubbing post.

Webb, the pistol in his belt, stepped into the foot loop and lowered himself over the edge. He had no qualms about the strength of the line. The *reata* was of braided leather that could, and no doubt had, stopped cattle and horses in full gallop. The maguey picket ropes were equally adequate.

"All right," he said. "Lower away."

Elias complied and Webb began to swing downward, using his free hand to fend himself away from the face of the cliff.

A man shouted from the opposite rim. "Let go the rope, you there, big man."

It was Jed Strapp's voice. In the next instant, a rifle exploded. Strapp, on the rim, had not waited for Elias to answer, but had fired.

Webb heard Madge and Loa scream. Evidently the bullet had missed Elias, for Sid Raines's voice sounded, thick with anger. "You fool! I'll do the shooting! We've got no powder to waste!"

The smoke Webb and Elias had seen had been the campfire of their quarry. But they were not quarry now; they were the hunters. They must have sighted Webb and his party, and had become the stalkers. They had been waiting on the opposite rim of the gorge for just such a chance as they now had.

A second rifle exploded. That would be Raines. Again Elias was the target, for if he were killed it meant that Webb would drop to death also.

Plainly, Webb heard the bullet strike flesh. But it was the voice of a girl that moaned in sudden agony. Madge!

The rope began to play out—fast. Webb dropped toward the rocks and landed with a jar among them. A rifleshot searched for him from the rim. It smashed into the cliff, fragments stinging his cheek.

That would have been Raines also. He would have had time to reload, and only he of the two could have come so close to killing with a snap shot under those conditions.

Webb crouched in concealment on the rockslide, the pistol in his hand, but useless at that range. In him was terrible self-condemnation. It was a repetition of the ambush in which they had been caught at the Virgin River and he blamed himself for underestimating Raines's alertness.

But this time it was not horses Raines meant to kill.

"Eli!" he shouted. "Eli!"

There was no response for a time. He could hear faint sounds above. Loa was talking, her voice high-pitched with strain, but he could not make out the words. Then he realized that what he was hearing was a prayer for Madge. A prayer in Spanish.

Stark despair froze him. "Eli?" he called again, imploringly. "Tell me!"

This time Elias answered, his voice dull. "It's Madge. She jumped in front o' me an' took the ball instead o' me. She saved my bacon—and yours."

Stark desolation engulfed Webb. A knowledge of an unbearable loss. A frenzy came.

He leaped to his feet. "Raines!" he shouted. "I'm coming over! I'm coming after you!"

He descended the rockfall in great, lunging leaps, veering his direction with each stride, for he knew what was coming. Both rifles flashed, but both balls missed, although the margin for one of the shots was deadly thin.

Before they could reload, he reached the stream. It offered little obstacle. It was swift but shallow and he raced through it and reached cover of the opposite terraced wall as the next shot came. It must have been Strapp again, firing in a panic, for the ball was yards away.

261

Webb began clambering upward, finding tough brush to cling to on the talus slope he was mounting to the first ledge. "I'm coming, Raines!" he shouted again.

Elias's voice, deep as a lion's roar, sounded. "An' me!"

Elias had slid down the rope to the rockslide. He came racing across the stream, water showering around him. Raines fired, but evidently he too was now nerve-shaken and his bullet went wide.

Webb continued to ascend the terraced flank. "Stay there, Raines!" he said. "This is for Terry! And for Madge Peary! You just shot her, you know! You shot a girl. I'm going to pay off for them. For the paymaster you murdered. For everything you've done."

To his left, Elias was also ascending the ledges in lunging leaps. Neither made any attempt at silence or real concealment. This was a frontal assault.

Both Strapp and Raines kept shooting down at them as fast as they could ram powder and lead into their rifles. But their bullets were finding only sound and shadows, for this place was full of echoes, full of the clatter of loose rocks and of tiny avalanches that Webb and Elias were touching off in their heedless ascent.

The rifles stopped. Webb, a few rods from the rim, heard Strapp snarl, "No, you don't, you yellow pup! You're not turnin' tail an' let me stand 'em alone."

Webb and Elias reached the rim together. Twilight lingered here, washing the land in a soft, mauve hue. The rims of purple mesas and buttes were still touched by the flame of the sun's afterglow.

Strapp stood at bay. He grasped Sid Raines by the arm, holding him helpless, forcing him to face this last issue, refusing to permit him to take to his heels.

Both were ragged and unshaven, worn and gaunt. The *jornada* had dealt harshly with them. Strapp's colorless beard curled over his great jaws. Raines was a far cry from the trim and handsome Dragoon officer of other days.

Their rifles were in their hands, but Strapp cast his aside. Their guns were empty and they had no time to reload.

But Strapp had a knife. Elias also had a knife. They moved toward each other without hesitation, as though this was a long-delayed meeting that both had known was inevitable.

Webb raced in and leaped at Raines before the man could retreat. Raines had a knife also, but Webb struck it aside with a blow from the muzzle of his pistol. He placed the pistol against Raines's chest.

He could have blown Raines's life from him. The desire was a madness in him. But now that he had him in his grasp after all these months and years, he could not bring himself to pull the trigger.

Raines grasped the barrel of the six-shooter. They fought for its possession. Then both preferred to settle this by hand. They both released the gun and fought with fists. And with boot and fingernail. With gouging hands, with knee and elbow.

Raines fought to kill, Webb to distill from him all the wrongs, all the bitterness that was in him. All the loss and the unbearable grief. Above all, to pay for the moaning he had heard when Raines's bullet had struck Madge.

They stood toe-to-toe, hammering with fists. They sought to strike and not to parry. They took blows to land blows. At times they were locked in panting battle, rolling on the ground.

And a few yards away, Strapp and Elias strained and slugged in a test of fierce strength, great muscles bulging, legs braced, jaws rigid. They struggled only a few yards from the rim of the gorge.

Raines clenched, using his knees in an attempt to maim. Webb drove the heel of his palm upward, smashing across Raines's chin, grinding teeth together and breaking Raines's nose. He got his hands in Raines's hair, twisted the man's head back. He would have broken his foe's neck, but, with convulsive strength, Raines broke free.

Raines seized up a rock and hurled it. It grazed Webb's face. Another rock struck him in the chest. He dove, catching Raines at the knees, sending his man crashing to the ground.

Webb leaped on him, knees first. His fingers locked on Raines's throat. And tightened. But his grip slacked off. Raines lay unconscious and bloody. There would be no victory in his death. He had to be allowed to live.

Webb turned to help Elias. The two big men stood braced on the lip of the gorge. Elias had taken punishment, but it was nothing compared to the chaos of Strapp's features.

Elias drove another sledging blow into Strapp's battered face. Strapp began to sag at the knees. He was completely beaten.

Elias grasped him by the waist and swung his weight above his head, holding him poised there, in a position to toss him to his death down upon the ledges below.

It was Loa's voice from across the gorge that saved Strapp's life.

"Do not do it, *querido mio!*" she called imploringly. "It is not for the lion to kill the mouse."

Elias turned and hurled Strapp away—but on solid ground near where Raines lay.

"That is good," Loa called.

She was on her knees, and Webb saw that she had been working over Madge who lay on a blanket near where the horses were picketed.

Something in Loa's attitude sent a wild hope soaring up in him. "Loa?" he called. "Loa?"

She arose to her feet, smiling. "There is no need for sadness, Webb Jernegan!" she shouted. "My sister, she is hurt very badly, but she will live to a very old age and have many children. She told me to tell you that."

Webb looked wildly at Elias. He handed Elias his pistol and left him to stand guard over Raines and Strapp. He descended into the gorge, mounted the rockslide to the dangling rope and mounted it, hand over hand, to the rim.

Madge lay ashen but smiling. The bullet had glanced along a rib. The shock had left her as though dead for a time. But now this was wearing off.

Webb knelt beside her and touched her hair. She took his hand and drew it to her lips. "Is it all over?" she murmured. "And you're alive?"

"Yes," Webb said.

"Thank the good Lord in heaven," she said.

Elias's voice came booming from across the gorge. "I found their camp an' horses in a draw close by," he said. "Look what I found in their packs."

He was silhouetted against the sky in the deepening dusk. He was holding high aloft a shapeless object.

"The bag of purty stones!" Elias said exultantly.

266

Loa began to laugh and cry almost hysterically. Webb and Madge looked at each other. They had almost forgotten the pretty stones in the stress of the pursuit.

When daybreak came, Webb recrossed the gorge and joined Elias who had stood guard over Raines all night. Jed Strapp was not in sight. Elias shrugged when Webb looked at him questioningly.

"I let him slip away," Elias said. "He thought he was being mighty sly. I didn't try to stop him."

Webb nodded. "That's the best way, no doubt. He might be able to make it out on foot, but he'll have hard going."

Raines sat, chin on his chest, all the spirit crushed out of him. Webb formed a noose from a picket line and dropped it over Raines's head.

"That stays there as long as we're together, Sid," he said. "Try to get away and it will tighten around your neck."

He returned across the gorge to rejoin Loa and Madge. It was nearly forty-eight hours before Elias was able to find a route feasible for horses and ride into their camp. He brought Raines with him, tied to his own mount, the noose still around his neck.

They camped there for more than two weeks before Madge was strong enough to travel. Then they again headed for Santa Fe.

Beset by the complexities of commanding an invading army, General Stephen Watts Kearny sat in the quarters he had taken over in the palace at Santa Fe. The date was August 20, 1846, and Kearny's forces had entered Santa Fe two days previously after a hard, overland march from Leavenworth. Santa Fe was now American soil. Kearny's next objective was California.

An aide entered, saluted and said, "Sir, a person asks to see you who says he was a lieutenant of Dragoons. He gives the name of Webb Jernegan."

Kearny stared, his thoughts snapping away from his own troubles.

"Jernegan?" he exclaimed. "Have you lost your mind?"

"Sir, this man is accompanied by a person who says he was a former scout for the Dragoons. Name of Elias Barnes. With them are two ladies. I assume they're ladies, but all of them look like they've had a hard time of it. They've got with them a prisoner with a rope around his neck. They say the prisoner's name is Sidney Raines and that he was once a captain of Dragoons. I can't make heads or tails out—"

"Impossible!" Kearny exploded. "Jernegan was convicted of Raines's murder. I was judge advocate at his court-martial."

He pushed past his aide and strode to the

door. Webb and his companions stood there, their horses in the background. Webb and Raines were linked together by the noosed rope. It had never been removed from Raines's neck since the day at the gorge.

Madge was with Webb, her hand on his arm. Elias and Loa were smiling.

"Impossible!" Kearny said again. But this time without conviction.

"Anything's possible, Colonel," Webb said.

"The commanding officer is a general now, and is to be addressed as such," the aide spoke importantly.

"I stand corrected," Webb said. "There are other corrections to be made. First on the list is the release of my brother, Terence Jernegan, from prison where he was sentenced for crimes committed by Captain Raines."

"You may be right," said the stunned general.

"He is very right," Madge said.

"And we will scratch out the eyes of any who tries to say he is wrong," Loa said.

"That's no way to speak to the general," Elias remonstrated.

Loa stood on tiptoe, placed her arms around Elias and kissed him. "I am sorry," she said meekly. "I will not do it again if you do not wish me to."

"I'm bewildered," the general admitted. "Just how many tails are there to this cat, and which do we grab first?"

"I'll turn the prisoner over to you," Webb said. "After that we'd like to find a parson. I have no doubt there's one with your command. Miss Peary, foolishly, has honored me by consenting to marry me. Later on, we'd appreciate an escort to Leavenworth, along with your affidavit that Sidney Raines is alive and that you recommend my brother's release and that Eli, here, by reason of innocence of any crime, and loyalty to his superior officer, be cleared of all charges. After that—" He looked down at Madge. "After that, you may not believe it, General, when we tell you where we've already been, but we still have quite a journey to make. We have an important matter to attend at a place called Goodhaven in Massachusetts. A matter having to do with some pretty stones."

Madge spoke. "And after that, General, I imagine that myself and my sister will probably come back to the plains with our husbands."

"Husbands?" Webb echoed. He looked at Elias, grinning.

Nobody spoke for a space. Elias kept swallowing hard. "I reckon the preacher might have a couple of other customers," he blurted out. Beet-red, he glared challengingly at Loa. "What do you say, slant-eyes?" he asked shakily.

Loa looked down her nose at him. "Is this a proposal of marriage, *si*?" she demanded. "If that is so, I wish it stated properly."

Elias was now too terrified by his own brashness to speak.

"Tell the girl you love her, you idiot!" Webb said. "Tell her you'll learn to be a gentleman, that you'll be sober, industrious and won't ever look at another woman and that—"

"I will see to the last of what you just said," Loa stated. "The other things I do not care about. She moved to Elias and kissed him again. "You are so big, my brave one," she cooed. "So very strong."

Center Point Large Print
600 Brooks Road / PO Box 1
Thorndike, ME 04986-0001 USA

(207) 568-3717

US & Canada:
1 800 929-9108
www.centerpointlargeprint.com